BABASAHEB AMBEDKAR: AN INSPIRATIONAL LIFE

Mukunda Rao is a novelist, playwright and thinker whose powerful writing explores India's greatest minds. A retired professor of English, he is the author of over 15 books including Babasaheb Ambedkar, Sky-Clad and The Buddha. His play Babasaheb has been staged across Karnataka. Rao's work reflects a deep commitment to justice, human rights and ideas that shape how we live and think today.

BABASAHEB AMBEDKAR

AN INSPIRATIONAL LIFE

MUKUNDA RAO

First published by Dr Ambedkar Memorial Education Trust, in 2000

Published by Red Panda, an imprint of Westland Books, a division of Nasadiya Technologies Private Limited, in 2025

No. 269/2B, First Floor, 'Irai Arul', Vimalraj Street, Nethaji Nagar, Alapakkam Main Road, Maduravoyal, Chennai 600095

Westland, the Westland logo, Red Panda and the Red Panda logo are the trademarks of Nasadiya Technologies Private Limited, or its affiliates.

Copyright © Mukunda Rao, 2000, 2025

Mukunda Rao asserts the moral right to be identified as the author of this work.

ISBN: 9789371979962

10 9 8 7 6 5 4 3 2 1

The views and opinions expressed in this work are the author's own and the facts are as reported by him, and the publisher is in no way liable for the same.

All rights reserved

Typeset by Jojy Philip

Printed at Parksons Graphics Pvt. Ltd

No part of this book may be reproduced, or stored in a retrieval system, or transmitted in any form or by any means, electronic, mechanical, photocopying, recording, or otherwise, without express written permission of the publisher.

PREFACE

This introductory book on Babasaheb Ambedkar was written in 2000, while working as a lecturer at Dr. Ambedkar Degree College, Bangalore. It was important to introduce our students to his remarkable life and work as a scholar of extraordinary calibre, a brilliant journalist, a social reformer who worked tirelessly for not only the emancipation of the downtrodden but also championed the cause of women's right, an educationist who founded the People's Education Society, the chief architect of the Indian constitution and reviver of Buddhism in India.

The book is now republished by Westland with some significant changes, keeping in view the needs of the young readers. I sincerely hope this work would be useful not only to them but even to those who are interested in the life and thought of Babasaheb Ambedkar. Needless to say that an understanding of modern Indian history, of Indian renaissance and the social struggles of the depressed classes, of even the freedom struggle and Gandhiji's life and work would be incomplete without an understanding and appreciation of the incredible life and struggles of Dr Ambedkar.

The credit for the publication of this new edition should go to Ajitha G.S who believed in the significance of this work, especially for the young readers. My grateful thanks to her and to Vidhi Bhargava for turning the text into a crisp narrative with engaging headers. I also owe my grateful thanks to Saurabh Garge for the cover design and Muhammed Lesin for proofreading the book.

CHAPTER 1

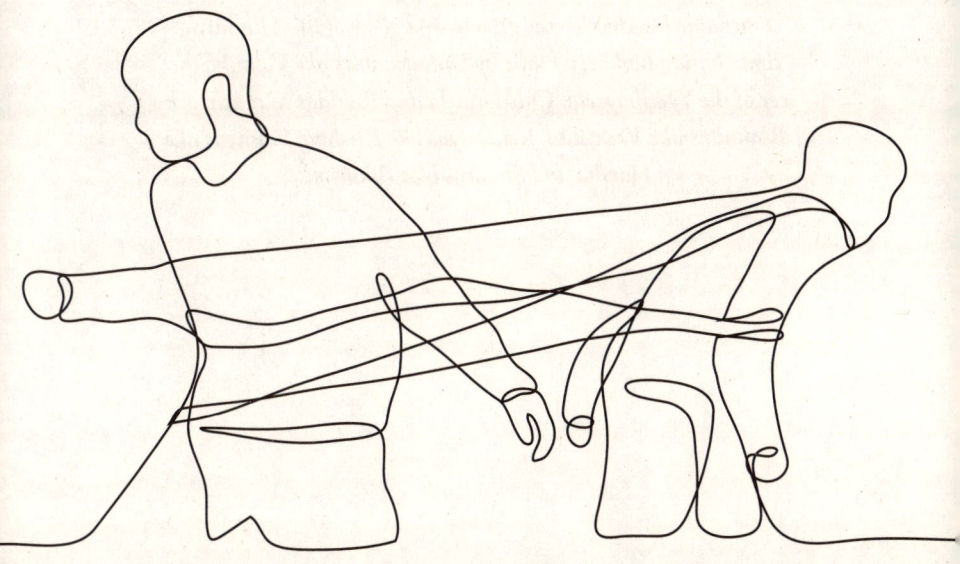

Ambedkar Reflects

As a matter of fact, it is your birthright to get food, shelter and clothing in this land in equal proportion with every individual high or low.

*

If you believe in living a respectable life, you believe in self-help which is the best help... We will attain self-elevation only if we learn self-help, regain our self-respect, and gain self-knowledge.

*

Hindutva belongs as much to the untouchable Hindus as to the touchable Hindus. To the growth and glory of this Hindutva, contribution had been made by Untouchables like Valmiki, the seer of the Vyadhageeta, Chokhamela and Rohidas as much as by Brahmins like Vashishta, Kshatriyas like Krishna, Vaishyas like Harsha and Shudras like Tukaram.

The Life of Dr B.R. Ambedkar
A Champion of Equality

The life history of Babasaheb Dr Ambedkar must invariably bring to mind the hideous practice of caste 'system' in our society. The words of warning he uttered some fifty years ago continue to ring in our ears but more loudly than ever before. Reflecting critically on the idea of Socialism or Revolution of the Socialists of his time, in his book, *Annihilation of Caste*, he warned:

> 'You (socialists) will be compelled to take account of caste after the revolution if you do not take account of it before revolution. This is only another way of saying that, turn in any direction you like, caste is the monster that crosses your path. You cannot have political reform, you cannot have economic reform, unless you kill this monster.'

THE CASTE MONSTER

The revolution has remained a utopia if not a myth, the monster of caste is far from dead, rather it still lives on and crosses our path in almost every sector of our life, be it domestic, social or political. If sometimes it takes subtle and almost invisible forms in private space, at times it becomes blatantly and violently political in public space. In a country where gross inequalities still exist, where more than fifty per cent of the population live in abject economic poverty, where more than seventy per cent of people live in villages where caste practices are still central to their lives, where caste carnage erupts every now and then, caste politics is seen as the only way left for the backward classes and castes to protect themselves and fight for their economic and political empowerment. And as regards the Dalits, their Dalit-identity politics continues to be the base and burden of the 'ex-untouchables' to critique social injustice, and wage their battle for what Ambedkar called liberty, equality and fraternity.

UNDERSTANDING THE CASTE SYSTEM

There are several theories on the origin of the Caste System in India. According to some, it was the creation of the warring Aryans who came from outside to keep racially different communities subordinated to them; others dismiss the notion of race and propose the theory that Aryans were one of the original inhabitants of India, and that caste developed as a result of very complex social, economic and political processes. Ambedkar himself held the view that caste system, in particular the degradation of the untouchables, was largely the handiwork of Brahminism.

> **The truth about caste**
>
> Whatever the theories of its origin, caste system has been divisive, violent and immoral and the consequences of it have been disastrous on Indian society.

History reveals that the practice of caste or the division of labour has never been based on or determined by the disposition or *guna* of an individual, but determined by birth. In other words, caste has been hereditary, strengthened or reinforced by endogamy. And the relations between castes have been largely governed by (often complex and contradictory) notions of 'purity' and 'pollution'. If a Brahmin is regarded as an epitome of 'purity', an ati-shudra is seen as the foot or the bottom or the lowest point of 'impurity'. Ambedkar called it a descending scale of contempt.

THE PLIGHT OF THE UNTOUCHABLES

The untouchables form the lowest stratum of Hindu society. They are variously called Pariahs, Panchamas, Ati-shudras, Avarnas, Antyajas and Namashudras. The *ati-shudras* or untouchables exist outside the pale of the caste system. Their social disabilities are specific, severe and numerous, so much so that their condition is most wretched to say the least. The touch and voice, and even the shadow of an untouchable were one-time deemed as 'polluting' by upper caste Hindus.

Untouchables were forbidden from

- Keeping certain domestic animals.
- Wearing clothes like the caste Hindus.
- Wearing gold.
- Using public wells.
- Entering temples.
- Accessing scriptural knowledge.

They were forced to, or conditioned to follow occupations and trade of a degrading order. They were street-sweepers, scavengers and shoe-makers and they continue to be so, even today. Some skinned carcasses, tanned hides and skin. There were untouchables who ate carrion or dead animals. The relatively fortunate ones tilled the land as tenants, or worked as labourers, most often as bonded labourers. Thus, deprived of social, religious and civic rights, they lived on the outskirts of villages in unhygienic conditions. Born as untouchables, they lived socially segregated and impoverished lives.

Having said that, it would be wrong to assume that this was so in every region of India and through all ages, that they led a subhuman existence without any resistance, as passive 'victims'. For there have been movements of great resistance, great counter cultures; and there have been personalities of extraordinary character and depth from this class of *shudras* and *ati-shudras*, who have all contributed to the development of what goes under the name of Indian cultures. Such a story or history, wherein the *shudras* and *ati-shudras* have not been mere victims, but have been masters and heroes of great cultural movements, needs to be written and highlighted as a corrective to the one-sided narratives that project Dalits as permanently oppressed, as passive victims.

MOVEMENTS AGAINST CASTEISM

From the time of the Buddha, some two thousand five hundred years ago, to modern times, we see several movements launched against the evils of caste system.

Historical figures who fought caste

- 11th Century: Acharya Ramanuja drew untouchables into his fold and threw open to them the monasteries and temples he founded and built.

- 12th Century Karnataka: Basava, a minister in the court of King Bijjala, developed a strong critique of the caste system. His was probably the greatest socio-religious movement against casteism, Brahminical authority, and old rituals.

- Succeeding Years: Saints such as Chakradhar, Ramandas, Kabir, Tukaram and others, who all taught a philosophy of **bhakti** that condemned caste discrimination and spoke of equality between all human beings.

- Narayana Guru (Kerala): Born in the Ezhava community, he challenged Brahminism and tried to change it through his unique interpretations of ancient scriptures.

- Socio-religious Movements: Started by Mahatma Phule, Swami Dayananda, Raja Ram Mohan Roy, all of whom worked to remove the stain of untouchability.

When Ambedkar came on the scene, the British, with their crafty political skills, had been ruling over India for more than a hundred and fifty years. The caste system, though fractured and subverted many times over through centuries, though under the British rule a Brahmin and a *shudra* had an equal status in the law courts, continued to be the operative principle of Hindu social organisation. At the time of the birth of Ambedkar, the untouchables numbered about sixty million out of three hundred million Hindus. And there were about three thousand sub-castes.

BIRTH AND EARLY LIFE: BHIMRAO'S BEGINNINGS

Mahars were considered to be the original inhabitants of Maharashtra. They were robust, intelligent, brave and virile. Ambedkar's grandfather came of a Mahar family, from a village called Ambavade in Ratnagiri district. Maloji Sakpal, the grandfather, was a retired military man. He had two children, Ramji and Mira. The family belonged to the devotional Kabir Panth. Kabir, who was a mystic-poet, condemned caste practices, and expounded transcendental *bhakti*, according to which, Rama, Krishna, Allah were only different names or symbols of the same God or Transcendental Reality. Ramji imbibed this philosophy and grew to be a religious man.

Ramji and Bhimabai had fourteen children, of which only three sons and two daughters survived. Ambedkar was the fourteenth child, born at Mhow, on April 14, 1891. He was called Bhimrao Ramji.

When Bhim was two years old, Ramji retired from military service and came down to Dapoli in Konkan, where, Bhim, at the age of five, along with his elder brother, started his primary school education. Soon Ramji moved to Bombay and found a job and residence in the military quarters at Satara. It was here, when Bhim was hardly six years old, that mother Bhimabai died. Ramji did not want to marry again, but he was to change his mind later, causing much anxiety and tension in the family. Meanwhile, industrious and religious as he was, he singularly brought up the children on firm ethical and religious footing, and saw to their education. In fact, Ramji had, for fourteen years, served as headmaster in a military school. It was but natural then that he was keen his children must be well educated.

With such a family background, wherein discipline and religiosity went together, Ambedkar grew to be an intense yet disciplined man, with great concern for the welfare of his people.

THE STING OF UNTOUCHABILITY

Thus, at Satara, along with his elder brother, Bhim completed his primary school education, and began his high school career with bright hopes. It was at this stage that he first experienced the stigma of untouchability.

Early humiliating experiences

One summer morning he and his elder brother had to go to Goregaon, where Ramji worked as a cashier in an office. Since he had not received their message, Ramji did not turn up to receive them at the Masur railway station. As the long wait proved futile, with great difficulty the boys found a bullock cart and started for Goregaon. They had hardly travelled a few yards, when upon knowing that the boys were Mahar untouchables, the upper caste Hindu cart driver dislodged the boys from the cart and abused them for having 'polluted' his cart and the bullocks. The boys did not give up, rather they struck a deal with the cartman. They paid him double the fare previously agreed upon, and the elder brother himself drove the cart, while the cartman followed them on foot, a safe distance away. The boys drove till late night without food, and when they desperately wanted to quench their thirst, none would offer them drinking water. The high-caste Hindus either pointed to some filthy water, or rudely asked them to go away. It was a shattering experience to the young boys.

This was followed by another rude shock, when one day, to quench his thirst, Bhim drank water from a public watercourse. On knowing he was a Mahar, he was badly beaten. Yet another shock awaited Bhim, when a barber refused to give him a haircut.

These humiliating experiences, and inhuman treatment at the hands of not only caste Hindus, but even the barber, must have made the young Bhim become painfully aware of the untold suffering of his community over the ages. And for anger to grow in his heart, eventually to become a great flame of indignation that would burn resolutely for over four decades, searing through the defence of caste-Hindu fanaticism.

Bhim was strong, fearless and pugnacious at times. One day, taking up a challenge thrown at him by his classmates, he walked to school in the soaking rain. Such was the determination of the young Bhim, although later, to his utter humiliation, he was made to sit half-naked in the class.

A KIND TEACHER AND A NEW NAME

But there was one Brahmin teacher who took a great liking to the boy. The teacher was quite obliging, kind and affectionate. On some days, during recess time, he would offer Bhim a share of boiled rice, *rotis* and vegetables from his box. The teacher's surname was Ambedkar. While Bhim's father, that is, Ramji's surname was Sakpal, Bhim drew his surname Ambavadekar from his native village Ambavade. The teacher liked his pupil so much that he changed Bhim's name to Ambedkar after his own surname, in the school records. That's how the name 'Ambedkar' stuck to Bhim; it was indeed a peculiar act of kindness and appreciation of the boy's personality by the teacher.

Bhim was doing well in his studies. He enjoyed a degree of freedom at home and indulged in his hobbies and fancies. For a brief period he developed a fascination for gardening and spent his pocket money on buying seedlings and new plants. And then for some time, fed up with the monotonous routine and studies, he cut classes to try his hand at tending cattle and rearing goats. Once he even did some 'coolie' work at Satara railway station, which of course invited strictures from his aunt.

A TURNING POINT: THE STOLEN HALF ANNA

Around this time, Ramji married again, breaking the resolution that he would never bring a step-mother home. Bhim resented the idea of another woman taking the place of his mother, and was repulsed at the sight of her wearing his mother's jewels. This appears to have been a difficult and depressing period for Bhim. He seemed to have hated his father for going back on his promise and marrying again. He was not too happy staying at home, and did not want to depend on his father for his maintenance and education.

He knew from his friends and sisters that boys from Satara had found jobs in Bombay Mills. Taken up by the idea, he planned to go to Bombay. And in order to secure some money to meet his bus fare and food expenses, he decided to steal money from the purse of his aunt who was, incidentally, dear to him and in whose company he slept on the floor every night. According to Ambedkar's own confession, for three successive nights he tried to remove the purse tucked up at her waist while she was asleep, but without success. On the fourth day, however, he did get hold of the purse only to be disappointed to find a mere half anna, with which he couldn't have gone anywhere near Bombay. The experience was quite nerve-racking and he was filled with shame at what he had tried to do.

Repenting over his foolishness, he reached another decision, which, in his own words, 'gave an entirely different turn' to his life. 'I decided,' he said later, thinking over the episode, 'that I must give up my truant habits, that I must study hard and get through my examinations as fast as possible, so that I might earn my own livelihood, and be independent of my father.'

It was a profound change in the life of young Bhim and he took to his studies with the zeal of a scholar, which was to last till his death.

EDUCATION IN BOMBAY: OVERCOMING CHALLENGES

Then came another change. Ramji moved his children to Bombay, to a *chawl* at Lower Parel. The place was predominantly inhabited by the labour class, that is, mill workers; also, it was then a centre for the notorious Bombay underworld. By the time the family moved to Bombay, the sisters had been already married and with their families they too resided in Bombay.

Bhim joined the Maratha High School. Studious that he had become now, under his father's guidance, he did the Howard's English Reader, and tackled translated works. These exercises enabled him to develop his vocabulary and have a hold on the language. And his passion for books (his father ungrudgingly bought books for him, even if it meant borrowing money from his married daughters), eventually, laid the foundation on which Bhim would go on to build his name as a writer of extraordinary calibre and range.

The next year, Bhim moved to the Elphinstone High School, which was one of the leading schools in Bombay at that time. Bhim now studied hard. The one-room tenement crammed with household articles, firewood and kitchen things, which at once served as a kitchen, a drawing-cum-study-cum-sleeping room, often noisy and smoky, and in the evenings a tethered goat bleating away, could hardly be a congenial place for any student to transact his studies. Still, determined to succeed, Bhim would wake up at two in the night and study under a kerosene lamp, till the break of dawn.

MORE CASTE PREJUDICE IN SCHOOL

The High School atmosphere, to add to Bhim's problems, was not entirely free of caste prejudices. One day it so happened that when the class teacher called him up to use the blackboard to solve a mathematical problem, there was an uproar in the class. The caste-Hindu boys had kept their lunch boxes behind the blackboard. Before Bhim could reach the blackboard, the boys dashed up and removed their lunch boxes from behind the board, for the touch of the Mahar boy was deemed to pollute their food. Generally the atmosphere in the school was quite discouraging and humiliating to the pride of a young, upcoming student.

DENIED SANSKRIT, EMBRACED LATER

To add to the insult, he was not allowed to study Sanskrit as the second language. Traditionally the *shudras* and *ati-shudras* were forbidden from learning Sanskrit, which was the language of the Vedas, and believed to be the language of the gods. So against his will, Bhim had to study Persian as the second language. Years later, Ambedkar took up the study of Sanskrit with the help of a tutor. For he could not afford to ignore the language which was a virtual treasure house of epics, politics and philosophy, of logic, dramas and criticism.

Notwithstanding these galling caste prejudices and insults, by dint of hard work and encouragement by his father, Bhim prosecuted his studies and passed the Matriculation Examination in 1907. This was indeed an event to be celebrated in a Mahar family. A congratulatory meeting was conducted under the residentship of S.K. Bole, who was a well-known social critic and reformer. At this meeting was another social reformer, who was also a writer in Marathi and a teacher, namely K.A. Keluskar.

He had taken a great liking to the boy and admired his studious nature. Keluskar spoke in praise of the Mahar boy's achievement and presented him with a copy of his new book, *Life of Gautama Buddha*. Four decades later, Ambedkar was to go back to the life and teachings of Buddha to find a new hope, a new refuge and vocation for himself and his people.

MARRIAGE AND HIGHER EDUCATION

In those days early marriage was a common practice among many communities. So then, when Bhimrao was hardly seventeen, he was married to Ramabai, a little girl hardly ten years of age. The marriage was conducted in the open shed of the Byculla Market in Bombay; the place where, in the morning hours, fisherwomen descended with their baskets, sat in a row and sold fish to a loud clamour.

The early marriage in no way affected Bhimrao's education. In fact, goaded by the ambition of his father, Bhimrao Ambedkar joined Elphinstone College in Bombay, and began his higher studies in right earnestness. Those were difficult days for Ramji; he fell short of funds and could not support Bhim's education, despite his great desire to see his son become a man of letters and distinction.

MAHARAJA SAYAJI RAO AND PROFESSOR MULLER: TIMELY SUPPORT

The timely intervention of Keluskar saved the situation for Ambedkar. Keluskar took Ambedkar to the Maharaja Sayaji Rao. He was a progressive ruler and had offered to support promising untouchable students for higher studies. Ambedkar was granted a scholarship of rupees twenty-five per month. Ambedkar was also fortunate in his teacher, Professor Muller, who was warm and kind and lent him his books and gave him clothes. But the general environment around continued to be bad and mortifying. The college canteen-keeper, who happened to be a Brahmin, would not give tea or even water to someone belonging to the Mahar community.

Undeterred by the humiliating condition, Ambedkar concentrated his energies on his studies and passed his BA Examination in 1912, with English and Persian as his subjects.

POLITICAL CLIMATE AND PERSONAL LOSS

During this period the British Government clamped down the fundamental rights of Indian citizens. Any act of protest or criticism of the government was seen as sedition against the government. Tilak was deported to Mandalay, and Savarkar to the Andamans. Gandhi was still in South Africa, honing his weapon of *satyagraha*, which, a few years later, he would use more effectively against British imperialism in India.

It was in such a politically oppressive environment, that soon after his graduation, Ambedkar joined the Baroda State Service. His father was not too happy. The offices in Baroda State were manned by orthodox, caste Hindus. To Ambedkar the oppressive and humiliating condition in the office matched the tyrannical state outside, and there was no alternative but to resign his post. To make things worse, around this time, his father, who had been his unfailing support and inspiration to his growth, breathed his last. Ambedkar's grief over his father's death was so deep that he could not be consoled for days onwards.

JOURNEY TO COLUMBIA UNIVERSITY: A NEW HORIZON

But soon, out of this sorrow as it were, emerged a new hope, rather a great opportunity. The Maharaja of Baroda thought of sponsoring some students for higher studies at the Columbia University in USA. Ambedkar took the opportunity and went to study at the prestigious university. But he had to sign an agreement to the effect that after the completion of his studies, he would serve the Baroda State for ten years.

Breaking barriers

- For the first time a Mahar, an untouchable, was going to study in a foreign university.
- It was to be an epoch-making event.
- Ambedkar had just completed twenty-two years.
- He had broken out of the limitation his birth in Mahar community had imposed on him.
- He could now change his *karma*. It depended on his effort, on his willingness to work hard, and his vision of life.

Thinking thus, he now addressed himself to the task with great rigour and determination. He studied for eighteen hours a day. The open and free environment in the university helped his concentration and resolve. None here would look down upon him because he was a Mahar, or even care to know to which caste he belonged to.

Professor Seligan, a well-known economist, was his teacher. Ambedkar now studied Political Science, Moral Philosophy, Anthropology, Sociology and Economics as the subjects for his course.

Academic achievements in America

- June 1915: Obtained MA degree for his thesis, 'Ancient Indian Commerce'.
- Next Year (1916): Read a paper on: 'Castes in India, Their Mechanism, Genesis and Development' – marking the beginning of his critical engagement with the caste system.
- Same Year (1916): Submitted his thesis for his Ph.D., entitled, 'National Dividend for India: A Historic and Analytic Study'.
- Columbia University: Awarded Ambedkar the degree of Doctor of Philosophy. From then on he was to be always referred to as 'Doctor'.
- Eight years later: The doctoral dissertation was published in London, under the title **The Evolution of Provincial Finance in British India**. The book became an extremely useful guide and reference material.

During his stay in America, Ambedkar had collected about two thousand books, both new and old. It was to become a lifelong habit with him to collect books, to browse through second-hand bookstalls in every major city he visited and buy books in heaps. These books on varied subjects numbering several thousands were later housed in a huge personal library he built in 1933-34, in Bombay. He was a passionate reader of books; a genuine bibliophile. A restless scholar, eager to know and understand every branch of philosophy and social sciences.

In his own words, 'For a man like me who is socially boycotted, these books took me to heart.'

Probably if he had not plunged into the politics of liberation of the downtrodden, he would have loved to live among books, spend all his life reading and writing books. However, the savant in him was forever alive and kicking, even in the thick of his political activism. And he was to go on and write books on religion, politics, social issues, law and constitution, and leave behind several unpublished monographs – most of which would become critical works of great significance on Indian history, Hinduism, epics, and the caste order.

FURTHER STUDIES IN LONDON AND RETURN TO INDIA

Ambedkar wanted to do more; the foreign degree and doctorate only whetted his appetite for more knowledge and degrees. In 1916, he left America to join the London School of Economics. But he could not complete his studies there as the scholarship granted to him by Maharaja Sayajirao was terminated. So he obtained permission from London University to resume his studies within a period not exceeding four years from 1917. And he did fulfil the ambition three years later.

On his return to India, Ambedkar was made Military Secretary to the Maharaja of Baroda. According to the bond Ambedkar had signed before going to America, there was no choice but to accept the job, although he would have loved to continue his studies in London and Bonn. It was not a mean post, though. But, from the day Ambedkar landed in Baroda, his problems began.

MORE DISCRIMINATION IN BARODA

The caste Hindus recognised or identified in him not the man who had achieved a doctorate from a prestigious foreign university, but a Mahar, an untouchable. No hotel or hostel would give him a room. At last, with great difficulty he rented a room in a Parsee Inn.

At the office, his staff and even peons treated him as if he were a leper. The peons stood at a distance and flung office files at his table. None would even offer a glass of drinking water, let alone share food with him.

EVICTED FROM HIS LODGINGS

Back at the Parsee hostel, one evening, a group of Parsee men, armed with sticks, stormed his room and ordered him to get out of the Parsee building. Although they were Parsees and they had no notion of caste in their religion, yet they too had internalised the caste prejudice and thought that the presence of a Mahar would defile their hostel.

Ambedkar appealed to the Maharaja for help. The Maharaja in turn referred the matter to his Dewan, who proved to be utterly unhelpful. Too disgusted by the insulting environment and with no help or support coming from any quarter, Ambedkar left Baroda and returned to Bombay.

EMERGENCE AS A LEADER

By now the Depressed Classes had collectively began to voice their protest against the evils of caste system. A series of meetings or conferences had been held and memorandums submitted to the government to protect the interests of the untouchables, to remove all disabilities imposed upon them in the name of custom and religion, and to grant them the right to elect their own representatives to the legislatures. The first All-India Depressed Classes Conference was held in March 1918. Not only members from the Depressed Classes, but also several prominent upper-caste Hindu leaders attended the conference and spoke against untouchability. Sir Narayana Ganesh Chandavarkar, Maharaja

Sayajirao, Tilak, A.V. Thakkar were some of the prominent members. At the conclusion of the conference, an All-India Anti-Untouchability Manifesto was drawn up and signed by almost all the prominent members, except Tilak.

BEGINNING OF A MOVEMENT

This conference marked the beginning of a large-scale movement against untouchability, which, in the coming years, would be predominantly led under the leadership of Dr Ambedkar. At that time, he was rather sceptical of the movement which involved caste Hindus, and which, sometimes worked under their guidance. However, Ambedkar did make a faint beginning of his political career by way of starting a weekly paper *Mooknayak* (Leader of the Dumb) to highlight and champion the cause of the untouchables. And he did participate in some of their meetings and spoke against caste tyranny. It was only at a later phase he was to take centre-stage and become the most vociferous and critical voice of the Depressed Classes.

At that time he was keen on completing his unfinished studies at The Grays Inn in London. In September 1920, with financial help, this time from the Maharaja of Kolhapur, who was incidentally quite notorious as anti-Brahmin and pro-British, Ambedkar went to England and joined the London School of Economics and Political Science, and also entered the Grays Inn to qualify as a Barrister.

LONDON: FOCUSED STUDIES AND HARDSHIP

In London he lived frugally in a boarding house. It was run by a harsh, insensitive lady, who deserved to be deported to hell, if Ambedkar had had his wish. His breakfast consisted of bread with jam, a piece of fish and a cup of tea. For dinner he had a few biscuits with butter washed down with a cup of Bovril. There were days when he went without lunch. Good food was not on the list of his priorities. Good books and hard work mattered most. He became member of all the major libraries, including the British Museum.

Though he was quite absorbed in his studies, he did write regularly to Shivtarkar, who was a close friend and for the next twenty years would be his right-hand man in all his struggles, inquiring of him about the journal *Mooknayak*, about the political situation, and then of course about his wife and children. But he could not be much bothered about the financial problems of the family. On whatever loan he had borrowed, he lived thriftily. He hardly spent any money on dresses, and often went without food to save money. He resolutely kept himself away from all forms of recreations, excursions, visits to theatres and restaurants.

World War I had started in 1914, with Germany declaring war on Russia and France. Three years later, America along with the British entered the war. By the time Ambedkar completed his course, Germany had capitulated.

Academic achievements in London and Germany

- June 1921: University of London accepted his thesis, 'Provincial Decentralization of Imperial Finance in British India' for the M.Sc. Degree in Economics.
- 1922-23: Spent a few months at the University of Bonn, Germany, doing further research in Economics.
- March 1923: His thesis, 'The Problem of the Rupee-Its Origin and its Solution' was accepted and he was awarded the degree of Doctor of Science. An

amplification of this doctoral thesis was later published as a book in London.

He would have liked to stay for a couple of years more in Germany and continue his research. But that was not to be. He had run out of his funds, moreover it was time to return home. Return to his people who waited upon him to lead their struggle against caste oppression. He was a different man now: grown in knowledge and experience, and stature. He was a Barrister, the qualification bolstered by a London Doctorate in Science, along with the Doctorate in Philosophy he had already earned in America. He was mature, and ready to inaugurate his struggle for the emancipation of the downtrodden. India awaited him.

CHAPTER 2

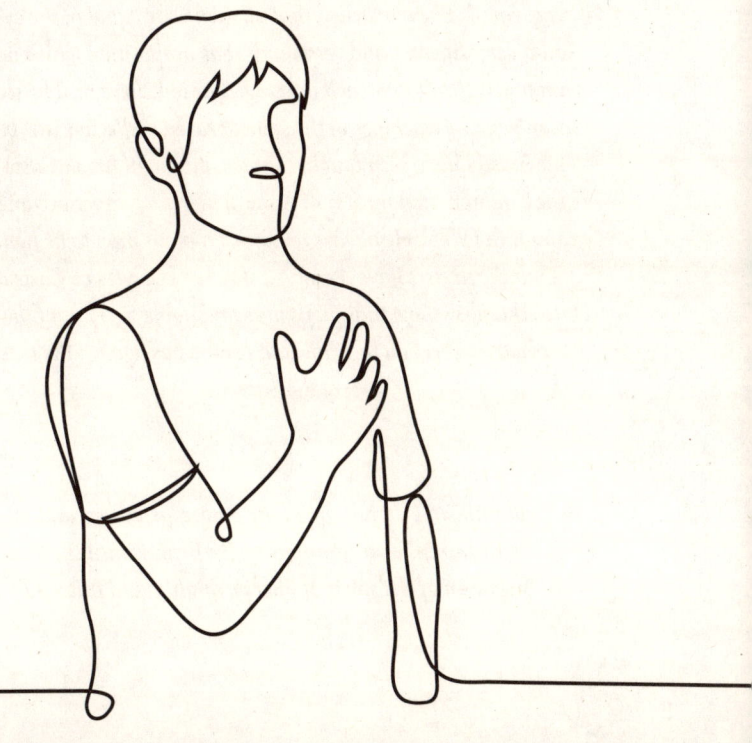

Ambedkar Reflects

History tells that Mahatmas, like fleeting phantoms, raise dust, but raise no level.

*

The saints have never according to my study carried on a campaign against Caste and Untouchability. They were only concerned with relation between man and God. They did not preach that all men were equal. They preached that all men were equal in the eyes of God-a very different and very innocuous proposition which nobody can find difficult to preach or dangerous to believe in. The second reason why the teachings of the saints proved ineffective was because the masses have been taught that a saint might break Caste but the common man must not. A saint, therefore, never became an example to follow. He always remained a pious man to be honoured. That the masses have remained staunch believers in Caste and Untouchability show that pious lives and noble sermons of the saints have had no effect on their life and conduct as against the teachings of the Shastras.

*

By Brahminism I do not mean the power, privileges and interests of the Brahmins as a community. By Brahminism I mean the negation of the spirit of liberty, quality and fraternity.

Social Struggles and Intellectual Engagements

Back in India, Ambedkar did not straightaway plunge into politics. Rather he could not afford to start working full-time as a social or political activist. He had no financial resources to depend upon; he had to find a job, earn his living and educate his children. It was a matter of time before he would storm the political arena with his trenchant critique of Hinduism and its caste tyranny, and launch his Self-Respect Movement that would change the contours of Indian politics and shake up Gandhi to commit himself more urgently and deeply to the removal of untouchability.

A LAWYER FOR JUSTICE

Meanwhile he made a humble beginning as a Barrister in June 1923. The Indian Courts as all public institutions and places were not free of caste prejudices. It was nothing new for Ambedkar, though. As a boy from his school days he had suffered caste discrimination. He was prepared, and it did not bother him much when a few solicitors would not have any business with him because he was a Mahar untouchable. He worked with whatever cases that came his way in the mofussil, till he could forge his own path to the front benches of the High Court. From then on he grew tremendously as a lawyer to be reckoned with. He won several remarkable and weighty cases, mostly for the non-brahmin community people. His experience as lawyer and his deep understanding of law and its socio-political implications would earn him the position of a leader of the labour class, later as a Law Minister, and then eventually as the chief architect of the Indian Constitution.

LIFE IN THE CHAWL

Ambedkar's lifestyle didn't change much. He still lived with his growing family in the same one-room apartment in the old *chawl* where his father had passed away. As a student, he had managed to study in that small, crowded room. Now, as a well-known lawyer and a rising leader of the Depressed Classes, he needed more space. But he didn't move. Instead, he rented another small room directly opposite the family room, which he used as a study and meeting place.

THE ROARING TWENTIES: A TIME OF CHANGE

The 1920s was a decade of great political ferment, as socio-political trends with far-reaching consequences began to develop. It was the period of great political mobilisation of the oppressed and exploited sections of society. The peasants, depressed classes, even women began to organise themselves into unions, sanghas or sabhas to voice their protests against injustice, and fight for their freedom and dignity. It was also the period when Hindu nationalism began to take shape.

In 1924, Veer Savarkar, who had been incarcerated in the Andamans, was released, and he was back in Bombay. Though

Savarkar continued to support the cause of the depressed classes and was for the removal of untouchability, he focused his greater attention on Hindu *Sanghatan*, to develop what is more popularly known as Hindu Nationalism. This communal politics, or what might be called the politics of Hindu identity, was to ignite communal feelings, unleash reactionary forces and create an atmosphere of suspicion, extreme distrust and religious bigotry. These fundamentalist Hindu formations and Muslim groups, feeding on each other, were to create the great divide, the almost irreconcilable divide between Hindus and Muslims, which was to eventually, tragically result in the partition of the country and bloodshed.

GANDHI'S FOCUS ON UNTOUCHABILITY

Around this time, Gandhi, who had been imprisoned after the debacle of the Khilafat movement, was released from jail. By then the Congress Party had been awakened to the gravity of the problems of the Depressed Classes. And Gandhi too, now well-known for his satyagraha, for the historic struggle he had launched against the White regime in South Africa, and who was considered to be a Mahatma whose heart bled for the poor, began to address himself more resolutely to the social evils plaguing the country. He made the removal of untouchability and the amelioration of the Depressed Classes an integral part of the Congress movement. For, in Gandhi's view, political swaraj or freedom would be meaningless and empty without freedom from social tyranny and economic poverty.

AMBEDKAR'S STAND: SELF-HELP, SELF-ELEVATION, SELF-RESPECT

But Ambedkar was somewhat cynical about the social movements started by non-Dalits. For he suspected, not without reason, that these movements were not geared to bring about changes in the power structures of the Hindu society, which should put a dalit on equal footing with a caste Hindu. In other words, the social reform movements started by persons such as Dayananda Saraswathi, Raja Ram Mohan Roy, even Ranade, Gandhi and several others, were all right when they concerned problems related to remarriage of widows, women's right to property, education of women, education and general amelioration of the poor and so on. But when it came to tackling caste tyranny, removal of all forms of caste discriminations, they were all not radical enough. They all began at the top and not at the bottom. The urgent task, however, was complete abolition of the caste system, and reconstruction of Hindu society on the foundation of equality.

Why Ambedkar distrusted other movements

- Not radical enough: They didn't aim to fully dismantle the caste system or change power structures.
- Started at the top: Reforms focused on certain issues but not the fundamental inequality.
- Hated Dalit dependency: Ambedkar believed Dalits should not rely on caste Hindus for their upliftment.
- History's lesson: Even saints preaching equality didn't create an equal society.
- 'No dust raised, no level raised': He felt efforts hadn't truly uplifted the Dalits.

Ambedkar hated the Dalits' feeling of dependency on the caste Hindus for their improvement. He knew from history that saints throughout the ages had taught philosophies and ideas of *bhakti* (devotion) that said all human beings were equal before God. But that remained a noble idea and couldn't lead to the creation of an equal society. 'Mahatmas had raised a lot of dust but raised no level.' And history had taught him that ultimately, injustice could not be removed until the victim or the sufferer himself fought against it through his own efforts and actions. As long as a slave didn't feel hatred for their victimhood or slavery, there was no hope for their freedom.

Self-help, Self-elevation and Self-respect were the mantras he offered to his people to encourage them into action.

'My heart breaks to see the pitiable sight of your faces and to hear your sad voices,' he cried in anguish. 'You have been groaning from time immemorial and yet you are not ashamed to hug your helplessness as an inevitability. Why did you not perish in the pre-natal stage instead? Why do you worsen and sadden the picture of the sorrows, poverty, slavery and burdens of the world with your deplorable, despicable and detestable, miserable life? You had better die and relieve this world if you cannot rise to a new life and if you cannot rejuvenate yourselves. As a matter of fact, it is your birthright to get food, shelter and clothing in this land in equal proportion with every individual high or low. If you believe in living a respectable life, you believe in self-help which is the best help...'

There were two enemies the sixty million Dalits had to face: one, British imperialism; two, the imperialism of the caste Hindus, or Brahminism. They could not afford to fight two enemies at the same time. There was no point in upsetting the British government while they had to fight for their civic, religious and political rights. Therefore, it was most important, Ambedkar believed, that they focused their energies on the struggle for the social liberation of the Depressed Classes. This stance of his drew heavy criticism from political parties and groups fighting against the British. But a time would come when he would combine his social causes with political issues and take a clear stand against British rule, when he would be praised as a 'great patriot'; as not merely a leader of the Depressed Classes, but as an advocate of nationalism and as one of the genuine leaders of the nation.

BAHISHKRIT HITAKARINI SABHA: A NEW PATH

So then, with his priorities clearly set in his mind, along with his co-workers, on 20 July 1924, Ambedkar founded Bahishkrit Hitakarini Sabha (Organisation For The Welfare Of The Excluded). The activities of the sabha were mainly in the Bombay Presidency; however, in the years to come, these activities would awaken the conscience and awareness of Dalits all over the country.

Objectives of Bahishkrit Hitakarini Sabha

- To promote education among the Depressed Classes by opening hostels or other necessary means.
- To promote culture among the Depressed Classes by opening libraries, social centres and conducting classes or study circles.
- To improve the economic condition of the Depressed Classes by starting industrial and agricultural schools.
- To represent the grievances (complaints) of the Depressed Classes.

By then, Dalit movements had gained momentum in many parts of the country. For example: Ad-Dharm in Punjab, Adi-Hindu in Uttar Pradesh and Hyderabad; Adi-Dravida, Adi-Andhra, and Adi-Karnataka in South India. What was common among them was their Adi-Hindu identity, or rather, their connection with Non-Vedic Traditions. And they saw themselves as the original inhabitants of the land, and Aryans as outsiders, attackers, and people who took over illegally.

THE ADI-DRAVIDA OR SELF-RESPECT MOVEMENT (SOUTH INDIA)

The Adi-Dravida movement, also called Self-Respect movement in Madras Presidency was, compared to other Dalit movements, quite different in its main thrust and ideology. For one thing, the movement here was not so much led by Dalits as non-Brahmins. M.C. Rajah, who was a prominent leader of the movement, was of course from the depressed class. He was to develop a close association with Ambedkar and work together with him in many anti-caste programmes. Later, they were to clash and part ways on the issue of separate electorates to the Depressed Classes. However, the Adi-Dravida, or the self-respect movement in Madras was spearheaded by E.V. Ramaswami Naicker, popularly known as 'Periyar'. Ramaswami was not a dalit by birth, but a non-Brahmin from a merchant class of Erode. He was a member of the Congress party in 1919, but gradually became disillusioned by its what he called Brahminic leadership. In 1925, he left Congress and formed the Self- Respect League in 1926. The growth of Hindu nationalism in the North, the equation of language and religion with nation (Hindi-Hindu-Hindustan) had a negative effect in the South, and as a result the anti-caste movement there grew to be not only anti-Brahmin, but also anti-northern and anti-Hindi. The northerners were seen as aggressors, as belonging to the Aryan stock, and the southerners as Dravidians, original inhabitants of India, unconquered by Aryan rule, with a distinct culture and language. The language chauvinism of the movement matched the religious fundamentalism of the Hindu groups in the north. Further, under Periyar, the movement developed a distinct atheistic character. To them, there was no god, no god at all. The one who invented god was called a fool, one who propagated god a scoundrel, and he who worshipped god was a barbarian.

Further down South, in Kerala, lived Sri Narayana Guru. Born in the Ezhava community, he strove not so much to fight caste-oriented Brahminism as to make Hinduism more progressive. If in 12th century Karnataka, the Brahmin-born Basavanna challenged the traditional, caste-based, Sanskrit-text-oriented Brahminism and developed an alternative path to Lord Shiva, in 19th century Kerala, the shudra-born Narayana Guru lived within the brahminical tradition as its critical insider. He simultaneously criticised Brahminism and upheld its liberating knowledge for human development. Unlike Periyar, or even Ambedkar, Sri Narayana Guru drew inspiration from the Upanishads and the Bhagavad-Gita. He spoke of a philosophy of life which recognised no discrimination of any sort between human beings, but saw and experienced all human beings, all creatures as one and fused with the supreme consciousness of reality or God.

The rallying cry of the movement started by Sri Narayana Guru rang a different tune; it was: 'One Religion, One Caste, One God'.

MAHAD TANK SATYAGRAHA: A NON-VIOLENT FIGHT FOR RIGHTS

Gandhi is recognised as a great apostle of non-violence, which certainly he was; probably the greatest in modern history. And the freedom movement he led against British imperialism was undoubtedly the most historically significant non-violent struggle known to us. However, it is not mere irony or paradox, but a lack of intellectual and historical correctness that fails to recognise the social struggles of the downtrodden as a non-violent struggle. Therefore, it is absolutely imperative to recognise and assert that through the ages, just as the women's fight for self-determination and dignity, the Dalit's struggle for freedom, for equality and dignity has been a non-violent struggle, involving immense suffering and sacrifice on the part of dalits. In this context, Ambedkar's struggle too has to be characterised as a non-violent struggle. It should be said here that there was more than a streak of non-violence in Ambedkar that eventually led him to embrace Buddhism which is grounded not only in egalitarian principles but also in compassion for all creatures. Ambedkar did offer the slogan: 'Educate, Organise, Agitate,' to the Depressed Classes in their fight against caste tyranny and injustice, but he never instigated violent aggression. He was a great believer in the non-violent, constitutional method to ameliorate the condition of the downtrodden, and to change the violent and cruel structures of both class and caste systems.

THE FIRST DIRECT ACTION

From this perspective, the Mahad Tank Satyagraha needs to be seen and appreciated as a non-violent struggle to claim the civic rights of the Dalits. It was also the first large-scale collective protest and direct action against caste discrimination.

In September 1923, S.K. Bole, a leader of the non-Brahmin party, had proposed a resolution in the Bombay Legislature stating that untouchable classes should be allowed access to or use all public water sources, wells, public schools, courts, offices and dispensaries maintained with public funds and run by government bodies. The Bombay Government issued a directive to make this resolution effective. But it remained just a gesture, even though there were several caste-Hindu groups and individuals who were sympathetic to the cause of the Depressed Classes and supported the resolution.

THE MARCH TO CHOWDA TANK (MARCH 1927)

It was time for direct action. At Mahad, on 19 and 20 March 1927, a huge conference of the Depressed Classes was held under the leadership of Ambedkar. It was attended by about 10,000 people from the lower castes, who came from many districts of Maharashtra and Gujarat. Ambedkar spoke to the delegates about the absolute necessity of rooting out ideas of high and low, and inculcating self-elevation through self-help, self-respect and self-knowledge. He urged the Dalits to re-tone their pronunciation and develop mastery over the language, to renounce eating carrion, to do away with humiliating and enslaving traditions, to abandon demeaning occupations, to acquire the forest lands and become agriculturists, to strive hard, educate themselves and enter government services. After the conference, with Ambedkar in the lead, the ten thousand people marched in a procession to the Chowda Tank, to assert their right to drink and take water from the public tank. On reaching the Chowda Tank, the access to which had been denied to the Dalits till then, Ambedkar took water from the tank and drank it. Soon the vast crowd of dalit men and women followed suit and vindicated their right.

THE REACTION AND 'PURIFICATION'

Within hours of this historic event, a rumour spread that the untouchables were planning to enter the Veereshwar temple. Gangs of caste Hindus, armed with sticks, attacked some delegates. There would have been a violent fight between the Dalits and the caste Hindus, but for Ambedkar, who appealed to his people for peace and discipline. He reminded them that they were there not for retaliation and revenge, but to begin their collective, non-violent and constitutional struggle for equality, fraternity and liberty.

A bitter controversy raged. The event evoked fierce anger and hatred in the minds of the orthodox, caste Hindus. Opinions clashed in the media, and among the political parties and social groups, and between those who were supportive and those who were against the direct action of the Dalits. Despite criticism, the orthodox, reactionary group among the Hindus, went ahead to 'purify' the Chowda tank. To the loud chanting of Sanskrit mantras by the brahmin priests, 108 pitchers filled with mixtures of cow's dung and urine, curds and water were immersed in the tank and its water declared free of 'pollution'. Later the tank was thrown open to the caste Hindus, even to Muslims and Christians; caste Hindus could wash clothes in it, even buffaloes and oxen could descend and take a bath in it, but the Dalits were barred from going anywhere near it.

BURNING THE MANUSMRITI (DECEMBER 1927)

This was nothing short of humiliation for the Dalits. It was a violation of the directive issued by the Bombay Municipality. A counteraction by the Depressed Classes became unavoidable. A counteraction that would send shock waves through the Hindu world and rouse the Dalits to intensify the struggle for their rights.

On 25 December 1927, under the leadership of Ambedkar, several thousand Dalit satyagrahis, most of them in rags, sunburnt, frail and weak due to years of poverty, gathered at Mahad. By then, the caste Hindus had filed a case in the court, and the matter was under judicial consideration. It was a tricky situation. Ambedkar did not want to disappoint and fail his people, yet he did not wish to upset the government. At last, at the request of the District

Magistrate, they were forced to put their plan to march to the Chowda tank on hold, as they had done six months ago.

Nevertheless, the conference passed a resolution to burn the Manusmriti, or the Laws of Manu, that imposed and kept alive the social, economic and political slavery of the shudras and ati-shudras.

The Laws of Manu governed the law and life of Hindu society. They were written nearly two thousand years ago, and orthodox Hindus still considered them reliable and important. The Book was a great collection of laws, customs and rituals to control and establish a certain social order in Hindu Society. It was a remarkable text in many ways. But it also showed, supported and established narrow-minded, intolerant attitudes towards women and shudras. The laws were extremely biased against the independence or self-determination of shudras and women, and upheld caste hierarchy as having a divine origin. To Ambedkar, Manusmriti was a symbol of inequality, cruelty and injustice. The open or public condemnation of the text had been long overdue. Hindu society needed a shock treatment, needed to be jolted out of its careless, cruel attitude towards its own people.

So that evening, copies of Manusmriti were placed on a pyre, in a specially dug pit, and to wild roars of anger and protest against the bigoted laws, the Manusmriti was burnt at the hands of untouchable hermits.

As expected, the burning of the Manusmriti created a great furore in Hindu society; and at the same time, inaugurated a lively yet sometimes bitter debate on the various customs and rituals in Hinduism that operated on the principles of purity and pollution, on the hereditary priesthood, and on varnashramadharma and its social implications. And the Chowda Tank case became a virtual legal battle between the caste Hindus and the Dalits, and it lasted for several years. The Dalits had to wait for another ten years, till

17 March 1937, for the Bombay High Court to decide the case in favour of the Depressed Classes and open the Chowda tank to them.

THE TEMPLE ENTRY MOVEMENT

By now the Temple Entry Movement had gained momentum in several parts of the country. In 1925, the Vaikom satyagraha had made Hindus aware of the caste prejudices supported and strengthened by religious authority. The Vaikom issue was actually not about temple entry, but about the ban on untouchables using the public roads around or leading to the sacred temples. A Syrian Christian and the followers of Narayana Guru had first started this protest. Later, many non-Brahmin leaders, including Periyar, were involved in the struggle. In March 1925, Gandhi too had travelled to Travancore to speak to the satyagrahis and support their cause.

There were about one million people belonging to the Ezhava caste, who were as cultured and educated as the upper castes; and the Pulayas, numbering 300,000, who were agricultural labourers, without whose labour the upper-caste communities could not survive. And then the Pariahs, numbering another 300,000, some of the products of whose labours were used in the 'sacred' temples. Yet, these low-caste communities, which formed one sixth of the population in Travancore, were denied the common, civic right to enter any of the roads around the temples. The controversy raged on, and the satyagraha lasted for several months before the authorities finally gave in and opened the roads for the Dalits.

AMBEDKAR'S APPROACH TO TEMPLE ENTRY

Ambedkar too took up the temple entry issue quite seriously and intentionally, but it lasted for only a few years, until he grew frustrated with it and realised that it couldn't be one of the priorities of Dalit struggles. In the beginning, it seemed necessary to awaken the Hindu conscience, to awaken the Dalits to their religious and social rights, and to change, if possible, the caste-Hindu mindset.

Moreover, as Ambedkar declared:

'The question whether we (untouchables) belong to Hindu religion or not, is to be decided once and for all.'

And he asked the caste Hindus, 'If you say your religion is our religion, then your rights and ours must be equal. But is this the case? If not, on what grounds do you say that we must remain in the Hindu fold, in spite of your kicks and rebuffs?' A religion that discriminated between two followers, a religion which treated millions of its adherents worse than dogs and criminals and inflicted upon them unbearable disabilities was no religion at all. Truly, the practice of untouchability had ruined the untouchable, ruined the Hindus, and ultimately the nation as well, he remarked. If the Depressed Classes gained self-respect and freedom, he pointed out, they would certainly contribute not only to their own progress, but also to the progress and prosperity of the whole nation.

In fact, if one looked at Indian history with an impartial eye, one found that Hindutva (the essence of being Hindu) belonged as much to the so-called untouchable Hindus as the touchable Hindus. And to the glory of this Hindutva, Ambedkar argued and tried to show, the untouchables had made as much contribution as the others. He cited the examples of untouchables like Valmiki, the seer of the vyadhageeta, Chokhamela and Rohidas, who had all contributed to the growth of Hinduism as much as Brahmins such as Vashista, Kshatriyas like Krishna, Vaishyas like Harsha, and Shudras like Tukaram. Therefore, 'the temple built in the name of Hindutva, the growth and prosperity of which was achieved gradually with the sacrifice of touchable and untouchable Hindus, must be open to all the Hindus irrespective of caste.'

THE NASIK KALA RAM MANDIR SATYAGRAHA (MARCH 1930)

While Ambedkar was preparing himself and his followers to launch satyagraha for temple entry; Gandhi, who was sixty-one-years old then, on 12 March 1930, started his famous Dandi march, or what is otherwise called Salt Satyagraha. Along with thousands of people who poured in from across the country and participated in this historic march, Gandhi walked 241 miles for 24 days, and at the village of Dandi, he picked a lump of salt from the sea and broke the salt laws. While this battle under the leadership of Gandhi raged high against British imperialism, Ambedkar launched his battle, using the same technique of Satyagraha, against what he called the caste-Hindu imperialism.

In March 1930, along with 15,000 volunteers that included women and children, Ambedkar led the satyagraha to enter the famous Kala Ram Mandir at Nasik. The mile-long procession reached the temple only to see its doors firmly shut against them. There were incidents of caste Hindus throwing stones and footwear at the satyagrahis. After a month-long struggle, a compromise was reached between the caste Hindus and the untouchables. It was agreed that both the touchables and untouchables would pull the chariot of Lord Ram on the day of Ram Navami. But the agreement was broken by the caste Hindus, who manipulated the situation and pulled the chariot without the help of the untouchables. Later, the temple was closed for the whole year. The untouchables had to carry on the agitation for almost five years before the doors of the temple were finally thrown open to them.

Because of these agitations led not only by Ambedkar, but also other non-Brahmin groups, including sometimes the

Congress people, a few temples were eventually opened to the untouchables, but there were many more which still barred entry to the Depressed Classes. However, Ambedkar soon lost interest in the temple entry movement. It seemed a futile exercise, a waste of time and energy. It was important and crucial to concentrate on the fight for their political rights. Moreover, Ambedkar had begun to think about changing to another religion that would offer equal status to the Dalits.

POLITICAL ACTIVISM AND THE ROUND TABLE CONFERENCE

Along with launching and participating in these social struggles for the social freedom of the Depressed Classes, Ambedkar had also been quite active in the political arena.

Early political milestones
- February 1927: Nominated to the Bombay Legislative Council, where he criticised unfair land revenue and income tax methods that hurt poor farmers.
- November 1927: Argued before the Simon Commission for the reservation of seats for the Depressed Classes in the legislative council.
- He demanded reservations along with adult voting rights, and if that wasn't possible, he asked for separate electorates for the Depressed Classes.
- He believed that if power was transferred to Indians, it would only shift from the British to the caste Hindus, which would harm the interests of the Depressed Classes.

By now, Ambedkar had become a significant figure and was recognised as the most articulate leader of the Depressed Classes. And in recognition of his leadership, in September 1930, he was invited to the First Round Table Conference at London, as one of the representatives of the Depressed Classes in India.

CHAPTER 3

Ambedkar Reflects

Most people do not realise that Society can practise tyranny and oppression against an individual in a far greater degree than a government can. The means and scope that are open to society for oppression are extensive than those that are open to Government, also they are far more effective.

*

The fact that machinery and modern civilization have produced evils may be admitted. But these evils are no argument against them. For the evils are not due to machinery and modern civilization. They are due to wrong social organisation, which has made private property and pursuit of personal gain matters of absolute sanctity. If machinery and civilization have not benefited everybody, the remedy is not to condemn machinery and civilization but to alter the organisation of society so that benefits will not be usurped by the few but will accrue to all.

*

My final words of advice to you is educate, agitate and organise; have faith in yourself with justice on our side, I do not see how we can lose our battle. It is a battle for freedom, for the reclamation of human personality.

Political Battles and the Poona Pact

The First Round Table Conference (RTC) in London in 1930, to look into the demands of the various parties and the minorities of India, and to frame a Constitution for India. The RTC consisted of 89 members in all. Sixteen representatives were from three British parties, and the other fifty-three members were all from India, representing various interests. As the Congress party was ideologically against the RTC and refused to cooperate, it had not sent its representatives. Some of the prominent members in attendance were Tej Bahadur Sapru, Jayakar, the Agha Khan, Jinnah, Dr Moonje, K.T. Paul, C.P. Ramaswamy Aiyar, Mirza Ismail and so on. The selection of Dr Ambedkar was seen to be of great historical significance for it meant that the British Government had recognised the interests of the Depressed Classes in framing the constitution for India. Ramsay MacDonald was elected Chairman of the RTC. All the members expressed their views individually and offered their suggestions; some spoke in favour of Dominion Status for India.

AMBEDKAR'S POWERFUL SPEECH AT THE RTC

When Ambedkar's turn came, he first spoke at length about the insufferable conditions under which the Depressed Classes lived.

The Depressed Classes formed one-fifth of the total population of British India, which was equal to the population of England. And then surprising the other members, Ambedkar spoke in favour of Swaraj, of replacing the British rule by a Government of the people of India. Speaking critically of the British rule, he demanded, 'When we compare our present position with the one which was our lot to bear in Indian society of British days, we find that, instead of marching on, we are marking time. Before the British, we were in the loathsome condition due to our untouchability. Has the British Government done anything to remove it? Before the British, we could not draw water from the village well. Has the British Government secured us the right to the village well? Before the British, we could not enter the temple? Can we enter now? Before the British, we were denied entry into the Police Force. Does the British Government admit us into the force? Before the British, we were not allowed to serve in the Military. Is that career now open to us? To none of these questions can we give an affirmative answer. Our wrongs have remained as open sores and they have not been righted, although 150 years of British rule have rolled by.' Then Ambedkar went on to show how the British Government policies only encouraged the capitalists who denied the workers a living wage and decent conditions of work, how it supported the landlords to squeeze the masses dry, and all this even though the government had the legal powers to remove these evils. Therefore, he declared, 'We must have a government in which the men in power will give their undivided allegiance to the best interests of the country.'

The great achievement of Ambedkar is that he drew the attention of the world to the depressing condition of the Depressed Classes in India, which was in many ways comparable to the terrible condition of the Blacks in America. By his graphic descriptions of the condition of the Dalits, he made the British Government become more acutely aware of and recognise the problems of the Depressed Classes, and prepared the ground for securing the rights of the Depressed Classes and their representation in Legislatures, in the Cabinet and in the Government Services.

THE SECOND ROUND TABLE CONFERENCE: GANDHI AND AMBEDKAR MEET

The same year, in August, the Second Round Table Conference was held. Ambedkar was again invited as a leader of the Depressed Classes. As a result of the Gandhi-Irwin Pact in March, the Civil Disobedience Movement, which the Congress had started, was called off. Gandhiji, Sarojini Naidu and Pandit Mohan Malaviya represented the Indian National Congress at the Second RTC.

Before leaving for London, Ambedkar and his supporters met Gandhiji. This was a meeting of great historical importance, as it marked the beginning of a long disagreement and debate between Gandhiji and Ambedkar over the caste system and Hinduism in general. It's important to note here that Gandhiji and Ambedkar influenced each other more deeply than most biographers have understood. This would have a big impact, though not always positive, on the political events that would unfold in the coming years.

Gandhiji knew that Ambedkar was quite critical of him and his programs for improving the lives of untouchables. So, Gandhiji directly asked Ambedkar why he was critical instead of supportive, especially when Gandhiji had included the removal of untouchability in the Congress programs and made it an important part of their agenda, and when they had spent Rupees two lakhs (2,000,000 rupees) for the benefit of the Depressed Classes.

Ambedkar said he wasn't impressed. Instead, he thought it was a waste of money because the Congress wasn't truly interested in changing the power structure, which was based on the caste hierarchy. And then Ambedkar said something no one had dared to say directly to Gandhiji's face before:

'History tells that Mahatmas, like fleeting phantoms, raise dust, but raise no level.'

Ambedkar had been deeply hurt and quite angry because some media outlets and Congress members had called him a reactionary, a puppet of the British Government, and a traitor. So, at one point, he got emotional and said, 'Gandhiji, I have no homeland.'

Gandhiji is believed to have gently corrected him, saying that he did have a homeland, and that based on his work at the First Round Table Conference, Ambedkar was 'a patriot of sterling worth.'

It must have been very painful for Ambedkar to repeat that he had no homeland. He then explained why he was no traitor and why the interests and freedom of the untouchables were his first priority. However, later in the conversation, when Gandhiji very clearly stated his opposition to the political separation of untouchables from Hindus, calling it 'suicidal,' Ambedkar is believed to have thanked Gandhiji for his honest opinion and then walked away in a huff.

THE DEBATE OVER REPRESENTATION

As the supreme leader of the Congress, which was undoubtedly a massive and well-organised party compared to all other parties combined, and being a Mahatma to millions of Indians, Gandhiji truly believed that he represented the interests of all communities and groups, including the Depressed Classes. He refused to accept untouchables as in any way different from Hindus. To him, the problems of untouchables were connected with the problems of Hindus and Hinduism as a whole. Therefore, the caste issue had to be addressed in a way that would stop the decay in Hinduism and help Hindu society regenerate. A political separation of the untouchables, he believed, would hurt Hinduism and harm the interests of the Depressed Classes.

By the same logic, he was totally against the separate electorates scheme granted to the Depressed Classes. In fact, he was fundamentally opposed to any special representation for any interest or group, whether Untouchables, Commerce, Labour, Landlords, Europeans, and other minorities, except Sikhs and Muslims. Hence, in the second session of the Second Round Table Conference, which started in September 1931, Gandhiji strongly opposed the memorandum submitted by the Minorities Committee, which demanded certain special political rights.

Furthermore, Gandhiji claimed that the Congress Party represented all Indian interests and classes, and forcefully criticised Ambedkar's demand for separate electorates for the Depressed Classes. Ambedkar was offended by Gandhiji's remarks and stubborn stance, and he attacked Gandhiji's claim to represent the interests of the Depressed Classes. Both during the RTC sessions and outside, Ambedkar sometimes went too far by ruthlessly attacking Gandhiji, his work, and his leadership, especially his right to represent the interests of minorities. The press in London gleefully highlighted this battle between the relatively unknown Ambedkar and the hugely popular Gandhi. Back in India, while Dalit organisations hailed Ambedkar as their hero who had dared to challenge the mighty Gandhi, certain sections of Hindu society and even some Congress members began to hate him and label him as an arrogant snob, a traitor and an enemy of Hinduism.

THE COMMUNAL AWARD (1932)

A year later, on 17 August 1932, Ramsay MacDonald, who was now the Prime Minister of Britain, announced what was called The Communal Award. It was a temporary plan for minority representation in the legislatures. The scheme offered separate electorates to the Muslims, the Sikhs and the Depressed Classes.

What is a separate electorate?

A special right for a minority group to elect their own candidates.

For example, a Muslim candidate would be elected only by Muslim voters, or an Untouchable candidate only by Untouchable voters.

This is different from a general election where a candidate can be elected by votes from different communities and religious groups.

In simple terms, it meant an electorate made up exclusively of Untouchable voters who would elect an Untouchable as their representative to the Legislatures.

The Muslims and Sikhs were, of course, very happy with the Communal Award, while Ambedkar and a few other leaders (though not all) of the Depressed Classes considered it a historic opportunity to empower and shape the future of the Depressed Classes. The Congress Party Working Committee neither accepted nor rejected the Communal Award, but Gandhiji was, as expected, quite distressed by the scheme.

During the second session of the Round Table Conference, if Gandhiji had accepted Ambedkar's right to represent the interests of the Depressed Classes, and if Ambedkar had cooperated with Gandhiji and they had worked together, they could probably have prevented the Communal Award and this unnecessary ordeal. They could have perhaps settled the issue by accepting joint electorates with reserved seats for the Depressed Classes. Now, taking advantage of the arguments and rivalries between and among the different parties, the British Government had driven a wedge not only between Muslims and Hindus, Hindus and Sikhs, Christians and others, but also between the untouchable Hindus and caste Hindus.

AMBEDKAR'S EVOLVING VIEW ON ELECTORATES

It is of great political significance and interest to note here that in the RTC, Ambedkar had not been too keen on separate electorates for the Depressed Classes as he had been for the reservation of seats for them in the legislatures and other government bodies. In fact, just three years back, he had been strongly against any communal representation. Speaking before the Simon Commission in 1929, he had said:

'Although I am for securing special representation for certain classes, I am against their representation through separate electorates. Territorial electorates and separate electorates are the two extremes which must be avoided in any scheme of representation that may be devised for the introduction of a democratic form of Government in this undemocratic country. The golden mean is the system of joint electorates with reserved seats. Less than that would be insufficient, more than that would defeat the end of good Government.'

But now that the Communal Award had been proposed, he strongly supported it, for he believed that the Congress Party, which was dominated by the interests of the high-caste Hindus and capitalists, would not be sympathetic to the cause of the untouchables. Given the separate electorates scheme, they wouldn't have to depend on the mercy of others, and it would surely help the political empowerment of the Depressed Classes. Perhaps his quarrels with Gandhiji had somewhat affected his decision, as well as his recent disagreement or differences with M.C. Rajah, a Depressed Class leader, who, along with Dr Moonje, had criticised Ambedkar's position and favoured joint electorates and reservation of seats for the Depressed Classes.

However, Ambedkar tried to assure, 'we mean no harm to Hindu Society, when we demand separate electorates. If we choose separate electorates we do so in order to avoid the total dependence on the sweet will of the caste Hindus in matters affecting our destiny.'

GANDHIJI'S FAST AND THE POONA PACT

For Gandhiji, the separate electorates were nothing less than a disaster. He believed it would cut up and break apart the nation without doing any good for the Depressed Classes. He was okay with separate electorates for Muslims and Sikhs, but not the Depressed Classes. The separate electorates for the Depressed Classes, Gandhiji said, 'will create division in Hinduism which I cannot possibly look forward to... Those who speak of the political rights of the untouchables do not know India and do not know how Indian society is today constructed. Therefore, I want to say with all the emphasis that I can command that if I was the only person to resist this thing I will resist it with my life... Sikhs may remain as such in perpetuity, so may Muslims, so may Europeans. But,' Gandhi asked, 'would untouchables remain untouchables in perpetuity?...I would far rather that Hinduism died than that untouchability lived.'

So, on 12 September 1932, in Yervada Jail where he had been imprisoned recently, Gandhiji started an indefinite fast (refusing to eat until a demand is met) for the cancellation of the separate electorates for the Depressed Classes. It seemed to many that Hindu society was on trial. The world's attention was focused on the frail old man sitting in a corner of the Yervada Jail. Anxious messages poured in from everywhere. Many temples in Allahabad were opened to the untouchables, and this example was soon followed in several other towns. Meetings were held all over the country, demanding the withdrawal of the Prime Minister's decision regarding separate electorates for the Depressed Classes. And appeals were sent to Ambedkar to break the deadlock and save Gandhiji's life.

All eyes were now on Ambedkar, who had, in an angry mood, called Gandhiji's fast a 'political stunt,' and had sarcastically remarked that Gandhiji's fast would have been justified if he had resorted to this extreme step for obtaining independence. Despite the appeals and threats, Ambedkar did not change his stance until Gandhiji's health began to fail and the situation reached a breaking point.

Several prominent leaders met Ambedkar and tried to convince him to withdraw his support for separate electorates for the Depressed Classes. Intense negotiations began, and at last, Ambedkar met Gandhiji in Yervada Jail. Gandhiji looked weak and exhausted.

'Mahatmaji,' began Ambedkar, 'you have been very unfair to us.' 'It is always my lot to be unfair,' replied Gandhiji, adding, 'I can't help it.' 'I want my compensation,' Ambedkar spoke directly. 'I am with you in most of the things you say,' reassured Gandhiji. And he asked, 'But you say you are interested in my life.' 'Yes, Mahatmaji,' said Ambedkar. 'I am interested in your life. And if you devoted yourself entirely to the welfare of the Depressed Classes, you would become our hero.'

The interview continued for some time, and at one point, Gandhiji pleaded, '...You are 'untouchable' by birth, but I am 'untouchable' by adoption, and as such more of an 'untouchable' in mind than you are... I cannot stand the idea that your community should either in theory or practice be separated from me... We must be one and indivisible.'

Gandhiji had no objection to the reservation of seats for the Dalits. Still, it took a few more meetings and much agonising, both over the long-term interests of the Depressed Classes and Gandhiji's worsening health, before an agreement was reached, commonly known as the Poona Pact.

THE POONA PACT: TERMS AND OUTCOME

By accepting joint electorates, Ambedkar agreed to the cancellation of separate electorates for the Depressed Classes. But as a compensation, he now demanded a much larger number of seats than what the Communal Award had given them (71 seats) in the Central Legislature. He demanded 197 seats, and after much negotiation, a middle ground was found to give 148 seats to the Depressed Classes.

On 24 September, Ambedkar signed the Poona Pact on behalf of the Depressed Classes, and Pandit Malaviya signed on behalf of the Hindu Mahasabha. Some of the other signers were M.C. Rajah, Rajaji, G.D. Birla, Sapru and Solanki. Gandhiji did not sign it himself, but he broke his fast, listening to the singing of his favourite hymn, *Vaishnava janato*, and sipping a glass of orange juice.

The Poona Pact apparently worked well for some years, and Ambedkar had no complaints. But he was to regret this decision later in his life and blamed it for the political failure of his party and his own defeat in elections. In fact, in the 1940s, he grew critical of the Poona Pact, demanded its cancellation, and asked for the restoration of separate electorates for the Depressed Classes.

WHY THE POONA PACT? A COMPLEX QUESTION

One might ask why, if he knew it wouldn't work for the benefit of the Depressed Classes, did he sign the agreement?

Was it because at that time he felt separate electorates for the depressed classes would be impractical or counterproductive? Was it an act of fear or pity? Fear because if Gandhiji died, it might, at best, end his political career, and at worst, cause a virtual bloodbath between caste Hindus and Untouchables! Pity or compassion because he wanted to save the life of the Mahatma!

However, as years passed, he felt betrayed when he realised that the Pact and the reformist measures had not led to any substantial improvement in the condition of the depressed classes, let alone their political empowerment. Perhaps, if the separate electorate scheme had been implemented for ten years, as Ambedkar had previously demanded, it would have empowered the depressed classes to bring about significant changes in their lives, to gain political influence and power to protect their interests. Or, would it have truly divided Hindu society, condemned the untouchables to remain untouchable forever, and proved to be harmful to their interests and growth, as Gandhiji had feared and suspected? The question is too complex to be answered in simple, black and white terms.

There have, of course, been opinions that the Separate Electorate Scheme would have energised and empowered the Dalits like nothing else could have done, and opinions to the contrary that it would have been disastrous both to the interests of Dalits in the longer run and Indian politics in general. However, just as Ambedkar felt betrayed and angry at what had happened, Dalits even today continue to feel hurt and angry, and are in no mood to understand the political circumstances of the period and excuse Gandhiji; rather they think it was a political conspiracy to subdue the Depressed Classes.

GANDHIJI'S POST-PACT FOCUS ON UNTOUCHABILITY

As for Gandhiji, the Poona Pact spurred him to focus greater attention on the removal of the curse of untouchability. In September 1932, the All-India Anti-Untouchability League was formed. Later, it was renamed Harijan Sevak Sangh, and Gandhi started a weekly called Harijan. The new name, or this new term for the untouchables, was meant to give dignity to the untouchables and to impress upon the caste Hindus to look upon Dalits as the 'children of God.'

HARIJAN SEVAK SANGH: STRENGTHS AND WEAKNESSES

Some Dalit leaders, including Ambedkar, thought this new term was an insult and criticised the mild activism of the new organisation. Harijan Sevak Sangh worked to remove untouchability, promote education for untouchables, encourage inter-dining (people of different castes eating together) and temple entry, and generally work for the development of the Dalits.

But the Sangh had certain built-in weaknesses and lacked the radical force needed to start revolutionary changes. Gandhiji had envisioned it as a way for caste Hindus to cleanse their caste prejudices, as a form of penance for practising the sin of untouchability. This 'Self-Purification' approach could hardly have started the much-needed social revolution that Ambedkar desired and worked for. It was no surprise then that the sanghas (organisations) were largely managed or run by caste Hindus, and the untouchables were hardly represented in the executive councils of the sanghas.

Gandhiji's philosophy of non-violence and social action required the 'victim(s)' of any social or political oppression to be at the forefront of any struggle for their freedom. The Self-Purification approach should have been combined with the passion and drive of the Self-Respect movement. Gandhiji's activism implied direct, non-violent action against the proven wrongs of society.

If the self-purification approach was to be prevented from becoming just a pious wish and gesture, from becoming a ritual of toilet cleaning (although it did have great cultural significance), from turning Harijans into objects in a purification ritual, it should have combined within its approach Ambedkar's fight for civil and political rights and the political empowerment of Dalits. This is because the Caste System in India is not only a structure of cultural values and religious practices but also a pattern of unfair distribution of power and wealth. In hindsight, it appears to be a failure on the part of Gandhiji's leadership, a loss of a historic opportunity to bring about radical changes in the social structure of Hindu society.

CHAPTER 4

Ambedkar Reflects

I consider the foundations of religion to be essential to life and practices of society.

*

Hindu priests are numerous and appalling. He is a clog on the wheel of civilization. Man is born, becomes father of a family and then dies. All along the priests' shadows him like an evil genius.

*

It is foolish to suppose that in the event of our conversion to Islam everybody from amongst us would be a Nawab or would become the Pope if we went over to Christianity. Go we may anywhere, fight is inevitable in store for us.

As Labour Leader, Critic and Scholar

Just as the caste Hindus didn't beg or care to seek admission into the social clubs and resorts run by and for Europeans, which often had signs saying: 'Dogs and Indians are not allowed,' so also, Ambedkar now argued, untouchables didn't need to beg for admission into Hindu temples. He boldly declared:

'To open or not to open temples is a question for you (caste Hindus) to consider and not for me to agitate. If you think it is bad manners not to respect the sacredness of human personality, open your temples and be a gentleman. If you rather be a Hindu than be a gentleman, then shut the doors and damn yourself. For I do not care to come.'

The Chowda Tank Satyagraha at Mahad, the Kalaram Temple entry movement, and several other social protests and struggles, including the Guruvayur Temple entry movement in Malabar, had shaken the very foundation of the caste system. They had awakened the conscience of caste Hindus and built much-needed political awareness among the Depressed Classes. But this could only be the beginning, not the end. There were bigger problems: the problem of 'bread and butter' (making a living), and the problem of political rights and political power for the Dalits.

'You must abolish your slavery yourselves,' Ambedkar urged his people. 'Do not depend for its abolition upon God or superman. Your salvation lies in political powers and not in making pilgrimages and observance of fasts. Devotion to scriptures would not free you from your bondage, want and poverty. Your forefathers have been doing it for generations, but there has been no respite nor even a slight difference in your miserable life in any way. Like your forefathers you wear rags. Like them, you subsist on thrown out crumbs; like them, you perish in utter slums and hovels; and like them, you fall easy victims to diseases with a death rate that rages among poultry. Your religious fasts, austerities and penances have not saved you from starvation.'

What the Dalits more urgently needed were higher education, higher employment, and better ways of earning a living. Their freedom lay in these things.

A NEW HOME: RAJAGRIHA

Ambedkar now began to play an active role in the debates of the Bombay Legislative Council. In April 1933, he went to London to attend the Joint Committee meetings, where he debated with Winston Churchill and explained his position regarding the Poona Pact. He returned to India a much happier man and with loads of books. For some time, he went back to being a lawyer and also worked as a part-time Professor at the Bombay Government Law College.

He still lived in the two-room chawl in Bombay, which was hardly a convenient and comfortable place for a man of his profession and standing. But he now had the means to build a house for himself. During his travels abroad, particularly from London, he had picked up some ideas and designs to build the house of his dreams. At last, after living in the chawl for nearly twenty years, at the age of 42, he built a house at Dadar, Bombay, and called it Rajagriha. He named it after the hill in Bihar where the Buddha had delivered many famous speeches.

The ground floor was used as living space, and the first floor was turned into a huge library to house the enormous number of books on various subjects Ambedkar had collected over the years. When at home, he would most often be found in this library, sitting among his 'unfailing friends' (his books), either reading or writing his future books. 'The Saheb,' as he was now popularly known even by his family members, had a 'home' of his own.

A PERSONAL LOSS: RAMABAI'S PASSING

The Saheb's wife, Ramabai, had something to feel happy about and look forward to – her children growing up in a secure atmosphere. But hardly a year had passed in that house when fate dealt Ambedkar a cruel blow. Ramabai passed away on 27 May 1935. She had lived most of her life in pinching poverty, taking care of their growing children without much support from a husband who was most of the time abroad, pursuing his higher studies, and then later working tirelessly for the welfare of the Dalits. She had been a deeply religious person, keen on doing her pujas and faithfully following all religious rituals and customs, like most middle-class Hindu women.

Though a thorough sceptic, if not an atheist, Ambedkar had been highly critical of certain Hindu rituals and practices, particularly the role of priests. Nevertheless, as an act of love and respect towards his wife, whom he sorely missed at this stage of his life, he let his son perform the funeral rites according to Hindu tradition, which was incidentally presided over by a Mahar priest, Sambhoo More, who had been his friend since his school days.

CONTEMPLATING RETIREMENT AND A NEW PATH

Ambedkar had by now become the Principal of the Government Law College. And just when he was getting used to staying at home, the loss of his wife had come as a tragic blow. He was in his mid-forties, and the relentless political activity had tired him. In July 1935, the news was that he was going to retire from politics. Then came the rumour that he would be made either a Judge in the Bombay High Court or a Minister under the new reforms. According to government rules, a judge could not take part in political movements. So it seemed that Ambedkar's retirement from active politics was inevitable.

It's hard to guess the changes that might have come over Ambedkar had he agreed to become a High Court Judge. The offer, of course, did not come, and he was to plunge back into politics very soon. It's quite possible that Ambedkar made his every move very consciously according to a plan. He wasn't a leader for nothing. He wasn't without strategies, though some of them didn't bring the desired results and sometimes made things difficult for him, draining his energy in unnecessary or avoidable controversies. He was truly a man of iron will, tremendous self-confidence, and pride, though sometimes prone to boastful claims and taking extreme positions. All the same, with all his flaws and strengths, he was a man of extraordinary intelligence, power and knowledge. Like Gandhi, one suspects that he too believed in himself as the only one.

A DECLARATION TO LEAVE HINDUISM

For some time now, Ambedkar had been hinting at changing his religion. It seemed there was no hope in Hinduism, no hope of changing the mindset of caste Hindus, or of changing the social structure of Hindu society firmly rooted in the caste system. It seemed that as Untouchable Hindus, they would have to fight forever to secure their right to drink water from public wells and tanks, for the freedom of wearing good clothes and using gold jewellery and metal utensils, for the right to receive education and to offer pujas at temples, let alone occupy positions of dignity and power. The Depressed Class people who had converted themselves to either Christianity or Islam had automatically overcome these disadvantages and gained equal status in society. So it seemed that the only way out of the wretched condition of the Dalits was to leave Hinduism and embrace another religion.

At the Yeola Conference on 13 October 1935, which was attended by about ten thousand untouchables, Ambedkar declared that though he was born a Hindu, he would not die a Hindu. And he urged his people not to waste their energies on temple entry satyagraha and similar social struggles, but to start thinking about moving away from Hinduism and securing an honourable status and independent positions based on equality with other communities in the country.

EXPLORING OTHER RELIGIONS

Religious leaders from both Islam and Christianity began to try to win over Ambedkar and his followers. Already, several thousands of Dalits had converted to either Christianity or Islam in a desperate attempt to overcome caste tyranny and their extreme poverty. In fact, both these religions that actively seek converts had been quite busy with conversion for several decades now and had drawn a sizeable number of converts from untouchable castes. They had their own schools, colleges and institutions, with significant political power bases.

If Ambedkar, along with his followers, were to convert to either Christianity or Islam, it was feared that it would be a crippling blow to Hindu society. But Ambedkar was not particularly inclined towards converting to either Christianity or Islam. Moreover, he believed that both religions would 'denationalise' the Depressed Classes (make them less connected to their Indian identity). Rather, he was more inclined towards Sikhism, and Buddhism too was not far from his thoughts.

Ambedkar's declaration shook the very foundations of Hindu society. A very large number of Mahars, who were his devoted followers, expressed their willingness to go along with him. The Chamar community, however, began to move away from him on the issue of conversion. Also, a few leaders of the Depressed Classes disapproved of his move and begged him to stay within the Hindu community and continue the fight for their legitimate rights.

Several leaders of the Hindu community made a desperate attempt to stop Ambedkar, particularly from converting to Islam. The Mysore State Government declared, for the first time in its history, that the Harijans would be allowed to take part in the annual Dasara celebrations presided over by the Mysore Maharaja. Coincidentally, the State of Travancore opened 1600 State-controlled temples to the Depressed Classes.

GANDHI'S REACTION TO CONVERSION

Gandhiji reacted in his typical style, saying that a change of faith would not serve the cause of the Depressed Classes, that 'religion is not like a house or a cloak, which can be changed at will. It is more an integral part of one's self than of one's body.'

Ambedkar was, of course, not in a hurry; he was testing the religious waters, checking the political temperature, weighing the pros and cons, and strategising his moves. He would take another twenty years before taking the final plunge. Meanwhile, he was not finished with Hinduism, and his quarrels with Gandhiji were far from over.

ANNIHILATION OF CASTE AND OTHER WORKS

He published a booklet entitled *Annihilation of Caste*, which was actually the text of a speech he had prepared for the 1936 Annual Conference of the Jat Pat Todak of Lahore, but which he could not deliver. Later, further exploring the roots of the caste system, he would write *Who Were the Shudras?* and *The Untouchables*. Just as these books were attempts to start discussions and debates on the issue of Caste and Hinduism, and to clarify certain ideas for himself, these were also attempts to prepare the ground for himself and his followers to finally leave Hinduism.

Annihilation of Caste was at once a strong criticism of Caste and an act of tearing it down. His argument was that Caste was not merely a division of labour, but a division of labourers. It was an inhuman system that crippled and stunted the growth of Hinduism and made its people weak, timid and vulnerable to attacks from outside. Chaturvarnya (the four-fold varna system) was a contradiction in terms, and Varnashrama Dharma (the system of varnas and stages of life) was practically impossible to practise and ultimately self-defeating.

Perhaps, the remedy, he reasoned, consisted in inter-dining and inter-caste marriages. But these acts, as long as the authority of the Shastras (ancient Hindu scriptures) were accepted and followed, would prove to be ultimately useless. Therefore, the only way Hindu Society could free itself from this harmful system and reorganise itself on the principles of equality, fraternity and liberty, would mean to free every man and woman, like the Buddha and Guru Nanak did, from the control of the Shastras, 'cleanse their minds of the pernicious notions founded on the Shastras.'

DEBATING GANDHI ON CASTE

There were different reactions to Ambedkar's ideas. It was widely discussed, appreciated and attacked. Gandhiji called it, 'Ambedkar's indictment.' He admitted that Ambedkar was a challenge to Hinduism and then went on to say that caste had nothing to do with religion, that every religion would fail if judged by Ambedkar's standard. He defended Varnashrama Dharma as a sound and meaningful philosophy that could not be linked to the caste tyranny, which he called an aberration (a departure from what is normal or expected). And he concluded his reply by asking if a religion (Hinduism) that was followed by persons such as Chaitanya, Jnanadev, Tukaram, Tiruvalluvar, Ramakrishna Paramahamsa, Tagore, Vivekananda, and so on, could be so utterly without merit as Ambedkar made it out to be.

Ambedkar's long answer to Gandhiji's short reply was sharp and ruthless. He questioned Gandhiji's defence of Chaturvarnya, asking why then the Mahatma, born in a Bania community, in pursuit of his ancestral calling, did not prefer scales (business) to law, and pursued the career of a saint-politician. As regards the saints Gandhi had mentioned, he agreed they were all against the caste system and led noble lives, but their teachings and lives had ultimately no effect upon the life and conduct of the masses, unlike the authority or teachings of the Shastras. Lastly, Ambedkar argued that the question was not whether his expectations or notion of standards were high or low, but whether they were the right standards to be applied while assessing the merits of a culture or religion.

THE INDEPENDENT LABOUR PARTY (ILP)

For the first time in the history of British India, General Elections were to be held in 1937, with a view to starting Provincial

Autonomy under the Government of India Act 1935. The Indian National Congress, the Muslim League, the Liberals, the Marxists, and several other parties got busy making preparations to fight the general elections. The Depressed Classes or the untouchables had no political party of their own to fight for their cause. They couldn't depend on other parties to fight their battles.

Formation and manifesto

Ambedkar took the lead and formed the Independent Labour Party (ILP) in August 1936. In its manifesto, the party emphasised:

- Rehabilitating old industries and starting new ones to create employment.
- Safeguarding the interests of industrial workers.
- Undertaking legislation to protect agricultural tenants from exploitation and eviction by landlords.
- Planning and promoting village sanitation and housing.

It was not merely pro-Depressed Classes, but a radical, pro-workers, pro-people manifesto with a leftist orientation. In fact, ILP led some major combined struggles against capitalists and landlords, along with launching many battles against caste tyranny. The most notable among these struggles was the anti-landlord agitation in the Konkan region of Maharashtra, which brought together for the first time the Kunbi and Mahar tenants against Brahmin and middle-caste Maratha landlords.

Electoral success and opposition to Congress

The ILP fought the general election in the old Bombay Presidency since the party was based and functioned only in the Bombay Presidency. Out of the 17 candidates put up by the ILP, 15 candidates won the elections. Ambedkar was elected with a huge majority, defeating the Congress candidate P. Balu, whose cause, at one time, Ambedkar had supported.

The Independent Labour Party, under the leadership of Dr Ambedkar, proved to be a formidable opposition to the Congress Ministry. Ambedkar spared no words in criticising the Congress: its Ministry, which was dominated by 'Capitalists' and 'Brahmins'; its policies regarding tenancy, the Anti-Strike Bill, and the Khoti Bill. It is important to note here that Ambedkar was largely responsible for introducing a Bill for the abolition of the serfdom of agricultural tenants. He also introduced a Bill to abolish the Mahar Vatan, under which the Mahar community had suffered for long, and against which they had started agitating since 1927. The Bill was not passed, and they had to wait for another 23 years for the Mahar Vatan to be abolished in 1959.

STANDING WITH WORKERS, DEBATING COMMUNISTS

In September 1938, the Congress Ministry introduced the Industrial Disputes Bill, according to which, under certain circumstances, a strike could be declared illegal and put down by the government. The bill was obviously against the interests of the workers. The Congressmen, who considered their right to freedom a sacred duty and a divine right, had failed to argue that the right to strike could also be seen as a divine right. Ambedkar called it reactionary, retrograde, and 'a mockery of democracy'. Incidentally, all the opposition parties opposed the bill. About 60 trade unions, along with the Independent Labour Party of Ambedkar and the Communists, formed a United Front and declared a one-day strike on 7 November 1938. It was the first and hugely successful strike waged against a popular Government.

At times like this, given his leftist views, Ambedkar willingly worked along with the Communists. For some time, he even tried to find common cause with them. But eventually, he parted ways with the Communists. The Communist Party, like the Congress Party, Ambedkar noted, was dominated by Caste Hindus, particularly Brahmins, and they had no idea of caste tyranny, or they didn't care to seriously address the problems of caste. For instance, among the working classes, the untouchables suffered the most. They were never given the middle-range or higher jobs but always the lower or menial jobs with very low salaries. Communists were blind to these facts, which were determined by caste factors. In other words, they never raised their voice against the prohibitive barriers that kept the lower castes away from the well-paid jobs in the mills or industries on account of the practice of untouchability. For the Communists, their political goal or some imaginary objective was more important than improving the lives of the workers.

As a matter of fact, in April 1929, when the Communist-inspired strike of the Mill workers of Bombay affected the untouchable workers most, Ambedkar not only openly opposed the strike and criticised the Brahmin-dominated Communists as exploiting the labourers for their political ends, he even went out and persuaded the untouchable workers to return to work.

AMBEDKAR'S UNWAVERING LOYALTY TO UNTOUCHABLES

While Ambedkar's anger and criticism towards the indifference of the Communists to the problems of the caste system and the deeper cause of the Depressed Classes could be accepted as valid and understandable, it should be noted here that his understanding of Marxism or Communism was largely shaped by his primary concern for the untouchables. He was a strong-minded man, and the cause of the untouchables was supreme to him under any or every circumstance.

Sometimes his uncompromising stance was not helpful in working with other groups or building solidarity with political groups and individuals committed to socialist ideas. However, it needs to be recorded here that for a period of time, he did try to build a united front to fight not only the caste oppression of Brahmins but also capitalism and landlordism, which in close connection oppressed and exploited Dalits and the rural poor. He was in favour of the Left and non-Brahmin forces coming together to form a radical alternative to the Congress Party and jointly working on issues concerning labourers, Dalits and the rural poor.

But that did not happen; and he grew increasingly critical of the Communists and distanced himself from them mainly because of their anti-religion stance, or their ideological rejection of religion. Ambedkar held religion to be absolutely essential in the life of individuals and society, and therefore an ideology that dismissed the importance of religion and religious values was suspect. In other words, he knew better than most how religion could serve as an opiate to the masses, how in the name of God and religion the most vile form of oppression and cruelty could be justified. Yet, he believed that religion alone, not politics, could give a sense of meaning and purpose to life, and that it held the key to the reserves of compassion and wisdom which lay buried in the human heart.

WORLD WAR II AND AMBEDKAR'S POLITICAL STANCE

About this time, the Second World War erupted in Europe. In September 1939, Germany invaded Poland, and Britain along with France declared war on Germany. Soon, the USSR and USA were to join the Allied Forces. The bloody war raged for nearly six years over most of Europe and parts of Asia, taking the lives of 55 million soldiers and civilians. It was to end with America dropping atomic bombs on Hiroshima and Nagasaki in August 1945, destroying the two cities and killing more than two lakh people (200,000), not to mention the several thousands who were injured and would suffer from atomic radiation in the years to come.

On the very day England declared war on Germany, the Viceroy, without consulting Indian leaders and legislatures, proclaimed that India was at war. This was followed by a number of orders restricting the civil rights of the people and reducing the powers and activities of the popular provincial governments. Many liberal leaders and political parties favoured unconditional support to the Government in its war efforts.

Though Gandhiji and persons like Tagore too were for unconditional support, the Congress Working Committee, headed by Nehru, objected to the Viceroy's unilateral decision. The committee declared that if the government sought cooperation, it must be between equals, by mutual consent, for a cause which both considered worthy. Since that did not happen, the committee declared that India would not associate herself in a war said to be for democratic freedom when that very freedom was denied to her, and such limited freedom as she possessed was taken away from her. This was followed by the War Resolution, which led to the resignation of the Congress Ministries in all Provincial Assemblies.

AMBEDKAR'S UNPOPULAR STAND AND 'ANOTHER LOYALTY'

This angered Ambedkar, who was for unconditional support to the British Government, for remaining within the British Commonwealth of Nations, and striving to achieve the status of equal partnership. He joined the non-Congress leaders in condemning the Congress stance on the matter. 'Patriotism was not the monopoly of the Congress,' he thundered, and he would not accept the claim that the Congress Party represented the interests of the people, least of all the interests of the Depressed Classes.

It was about this time, before the Congress Ministries resigned from the Bombay Legislature in accordance with their War Resolution, that Ambedkar, speaking to the members of the House, explained his position and his politics in clear terms. Parts of this long speech deserve to be recorded here, if only to understand his impatience with other leaders of the Depressed Classes, his suspicion of Congress politics, and his strong and uncompromising commitment to the cause of the untouchables.

'I know my position has not been understood properly in the country,' he said with sadness. 'It has often been misunderstood. Let me, therefore, take this opportunity to clarify my position. I say that whenever there has been a conflict between my personal interests and the interests of the country as a whole, I have always placed the claims of the country above my personal claims. I have never pursued the path of private gain. If I had played my cards well, as others do, I might have been in some other place. I do not want to say about it, but I did not do it...so far as the demands of the country are concerned, I have never lagged behind...'

But then, he continued with a powerful declaration:

> '... But I will also leave no doubt in the minds of the people of this country that I have another loyalty to which I am bound and which I can never forsake. That loyalty is the community of Untouchables, in which I am born, to which I belong, and which I hope I shall never desert. And I say this to this House as strongly as I possibly can, that whenever there is conflict of interests between the country and the Untouchables, so

far as I am concerned, the Untouchables' interests will take precedence over the interest of the country. I am not going to support a tyrannising majority simply because it happens to speak in the name of the country. I am not going to support a party because it happens to speak in the name of the country. I shall not do that. Let everybody here and everywhere understand that that is my position. As between the country and myself, the country will have precedence, as between the country and the Depressed Classes, the Depressed Classes will have precedence and the country will have no precedence.'

This bold statement cemented Ambedkar's role as the unwavering champion of the Depressed Classes, willing to prioritise their interests above all else.

CHAPTER 5

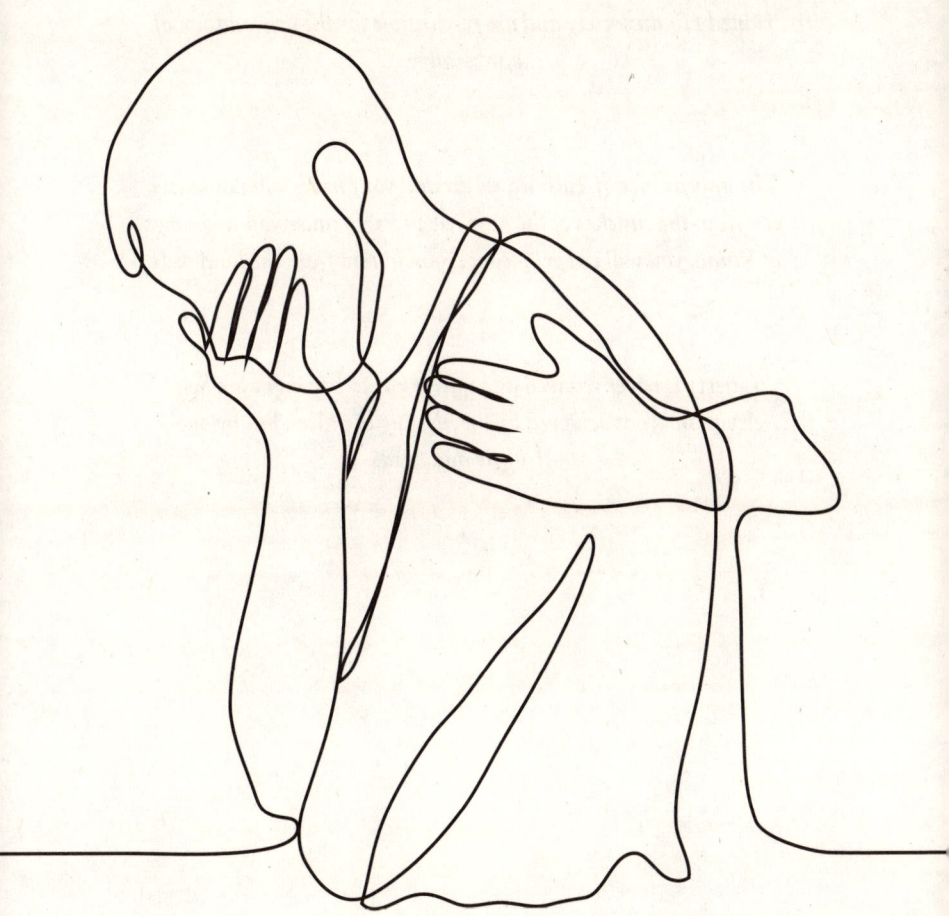

Ambedkar Reflects

These ideas of hero-worship, deification, neglect of duty have ruined Hindu society and are responsible for the degradation of our country.

*

The appearance of Tulsi leaves around your neck, will not relieve you from the clutches of the moneylenders. Because you sing songs of Rama, you will not get a concession in rent from the landlords.

*

Liberty is never received as a gift; it has to be fought for. Self-elevation is not achieved by the blessing of others, but by one's struggle and deed.

*

Thoughts on Pakistan and the Cause of the Depressed Classes

AMBEDKAR'S CALL TO UNTOUCHABLES

Ambedkar began to tour districts and address large gatherings of untouchables about the uncertainty of the coming days. Given their wretched condition, he said, it was not advisable for them to concentrate all their energies on political independence and forget the more important social and economic problems. A resurgent new society could be built only on modern lines, on the principles of liberty, equality and fraternity.

He advised the ragged men and women to keep themselves clean, keep away from vices, give education to children, remove from them the feeling of inferiority and instil ambition in their minds. He warned them against early marriage, not to impose it upon their children unless and until they were financially sound.

'Educate, agitate and organise'

He offered them the famous motto: 'Educate, Agitate and Organise', and carry on the battle for freedom, for the reclamation of human personality.

POLITICAL CLIMATE AND THE WAR

Meanwhile the political situation became serious and unpredictable. The Muslim League passed a resolution demanding the creation of independent states in the North-West and Eastern parts of India where Muslims were in a majority. The Congress grew wary of the Muslim League and warned Britain against any attempt to divide or split the country.

In April 1940, Germany overran the low countries such as Denmark, Netherlands and Belgium. In Britain, a coalition Government was formed under the Premiership of Winston Churchill, who as always, was aggressively opposed to transfer of power to India. Considering the gravity of the situation under war, the Congress offered cooperation in war efforts, provided a fully representative National Government was formed at the centre. Jinnah, who was the leader of the Muslim League, fumed and ranted, fearing a permanent Hindu majority at the centre.

SUBHAS CHANDRA BOSE'S EFFORTS

It was about this time that Subhas Chandra Bose, who had been dislodged from the Congress presidentship, planned to render a deathblow to the British power struggling to survive the war against Germany. He met Jinnah, Ambedkar, Savarkar and other prominent leaders. Later, he was to negotiate with the Japanese Forces to plan the possibility of fighting a war of independence against the British.

In October 1940, when already the bomb plot to kill Hitler by German Generals had failed, when Yugoslavs and Soviets had entered Belgrade; in India, after the frustrating and fruitless meetings with the Viceroy Lord Linlithgow, Gandhiji started individual non-violent non-cooperation against the British. He went from village to village on foot, delivering anti-war speeches. He was arrested and sentenced to three months imprisonment; soon to be followed by many leaders of the Congress, including Nehru.

Ambedkar's view on pacifism

Ambedkar's reaction to the situation was critical and caustic.

'Mr. Gandhi and all pacifists and believers in non-violence,' he said bitingly, 'will do a lasting service to humanity if they went on fast unto death when peace is announced, if the terms of peace offered to the vanquished are ignoble and unjust. The pacifist, it seems to me, has misunderstood his mission. His fight must be against a base peace and not against force. By calling upon people to abjure the use of force, the pacifist is only helping those who will insist on using force to victory.'

AMBEDKAR'S 'THOUGHTS ON PAKISTAN'

The same year Ambedkar wrote *Thoughts on Pakistan*, which was like pouring ghee to the fire as they say, to the already increasing communal passion and strife between Hindus and Muslims. Considering the fact that it was written seven years before the partition took place in a virtual bloodbath, it was a forewarning, almost prophetic in its anticipation of wholesale killings if the separation was not transacted through negotiation and peaceful means.

In point of fact, the book did not predict nor warn against partition. Rather, ironical as it might seem coming from a Depressed Class leader, the book suggested separation of Pakistan from India as the only way out of the destructive communal politics and bloodshed. Ambedkar foresaw those sections of Muslims, under the influence of the Muslim League and Jinnah, would never adopt India as their Motherland. The predominant interest of Muslims was religion, not democracy, he wrote. The Brotherhood of Muslims was not brotherhood of men, but brotherhood of Muslims and Muslims only. He even suggested total exchange of Hindus and Muslims between India and Pakistan. Only division, he argued, could help develop a strong Central Government.

Reception of the book

The book came as a jolt, it both confused and enraged the minds of many leaders. Though the book was quite harsh and critical of the religious and cultural politics of the Muslims, the Muslim League leaders saw in Ambedkar a staunch supporter for their two-nation theory.

AMBEDKAR JOINS THE VICEROY'S EXECUTIVE COUNCIL

In July 1942, the Viceroy expanded his Executive Council. There were now 14 Indians including Dr Ambedkar, as against 5 Europeans in the council. It was for the first time an untouchable was appointed a member in the Executive Council of the Government of India. Ambedkar had just completed fifty years.

The occasion was celebrated by the depressed classes in several places. Many Mahar institutions and groups organised a nine-day celebration consisting of flag salutation, processions and public meetings. Wherever he went thousands of people gave their leader, their Saheb, a thunderous ovation. On his becoming a Labour Member, congratulatory messages poured from everywhere, and felicitations were showered on the leader by people cutting across party lines, for his great achievements and selfless services to the cause of the underdogs.

The Quit India Movement

The Second World War still raged all over Europe. Japan had already occupied Philippines. And when Rangoon fell, Japan was knocking at the gates of India, which virtually pushed India into the front line of the battle. The Congress passed a resolution which said that Britain, not only in the interest of India, but also for its own safety, and for the sake of world peace and freedom, it must abandon her hold on India. It is on the basis of Independence alone that India would deal with Britain or other nations. It was argued that British presence in India worked as an incentive for the Japanese attack. If the British wisely decided to leave, India would manage her affairs in the best way she could.

On 8 August 1942, the Indian National Congress, under the leadership of Gandhiji, launched the Quit India movement, demanding immediate withdrawal of the British Power.

GANDHIJI'S CALL TO ACTION

Gandhiji told the people, '... Every one of you should, from this moment, consider yourself a free man or woman and even act as if you are free and no longer under the heel of this imperialism ...'

The clarion call stirred the imagination of the people, but it had its critics. The Viceroy had warned to crush the Congress if it dared to throw an open challenge to the government. Now, he did: repressive measures were unleashed, sweeping powers were conferred on the executive to arrest, detain and control, to confiscate money, documents, buildings, to ban dramatic performances, censor posts and telegraphy, to impose curfew and take action to crush the movement. Gandhiji was arrested and detained in Agha Khan Palace, and several prominent leaders of the Congress were rounded up and thrown into different prisons.

The Quit India movement shook the British power and plunged the country into an unprecedented turmoil.

Ambedkar's stance on Quit India

Ambedkar disapproved, thought of it as unwise and premature. The Muslim League remained aloof, watching the turmoil and so did the Hindu Mahasabha. Ambedkar continued to work as a labour member.

'Ranade, Gandhi and Jinnah'

On 19 January 1944, he was invited to Poona to address a meeting on the occasion of the birth anniversary of Ranade. The speech was later published as a book entitled: ***Ranade, Gandhi and Jinnah***.

Ambedkar held the view that Ranade was a great social reformer, who fitted the definition of great man, who had vitalised the conscience of the Hindu society and struggled relentlessly against social injustices. Comparing Gandhi and Jinnah with Ranade, he called the two leaders' egotists. He criticised the two leaders for making a mess of Indian politics and making it a matter of personal feud. In his anger he was quite harsh to dub Gandhiji's non-violent struggles as attempts calculated for personal ascendancy.

FAMINE AND AMBEDKAR'S UNWAVERING POSITION

The impact of the war on the economy of the country was disastrous. Several parts of the country reeled under famine. Gandhiji started on a twenty-one-day fast on 10 February 1943. This led to intense agitation all over the country, and thousands of people courted arrest, demanding Gandhiji's release from jail.

Three members of the Viceroy's Executive Council resigned in protest, but Ambedkar, along with Srivastava, remained unmoved.

Ambedkar was of the firm view that the Government's drastic action in 1942 was justifiable, otherwise, he reasoned, India would have been overrun by the Japanese. This stance alienated him further from the political groups fighting for Independence.

Continued efforts for depressed classes

Unfazed, Ambedkar toured many places, rousing the untouchables to fight for their rights. In one of the speeches he said that no country in the ancient past had such a tremendous and dynamic political life as the ancient Indians, but Brahminism with its caste system had destroyed it all. He visited Madras and met E.V. Ramaswami Naicker. He founded the Scheduled Castes Federation, and strove to build the party on a war footing. And then, as always, he never tired of seeking assurance from the Government for the safeguard of the interests of the Depressed Classes in the Special Treaty which was to be signed by the British Government and the Constituent Assembly.

POST-WAR POLITICS AND ELECTIONS

The Second World War came to an end in May 1945 when Germany surrendered to the Allied Forces. Meanwhile The Indian National Army, under the command of Subhas Chandra Bose, was crushed by the British troops. In August, with the dropping of the atom bombs on Hiroshima and Nagasaki, Japan surrendered.

In India, the Government revoked the repressive measures. The Wavell Plan in June 1945, was followed by the Simla Conference to end the political deadlock. The pattern of Indian politics began to change drastically. By then the Labour Government had come to power in England.

> ### General elections and safeguards
>
> Lord Wavell announced general elections to the Central and Provincial Legislatures. Ambedkar proposed weightage to be given to the minority's communities in their representation in the legislatures. He spoke for a united India, but for Dominion Status as against Independence, for he feared that the scheduled castes were still not in a position of power to safeguard their interests.
>
> In March 1946, when the British Cabinet Delegates arrived, he submitted a memorandum before the Cabinet Mission for separate electorates for the Scheduled Castes. It also included safeguards such as a new settlement, adequate representation in the legislatures and executives, public services and public service commissions.

Independence was now round the corner, and Ambedkar got increasingly worked up over the future of the scheduled castes in Independent India. He even went to London briefly, to plead for the constitutional safeguards for the scheduled castes.

THE ALL-INDIA SCHEDULED CASTES FEDERATION

Back from London, he plunged into the election campaign. The old ILP-Independent Labour Party had been changed into The All-India Scheduled Castes Federation (AISCF). In his speeches he emphasized that the Scheduled Castes, like the Muslim League, were not for territorial division of the country, not for patronage of any kind, but for equal rights, and for a constitution that would safeguard their interests and would be framed with their approval.

However, in the general elections, the AISCF was completely routed. Even Ambedkar had to face defeat, and he had no clue why they failed so miserably. It was a stunning blow. He went into despair, and began to grope for drastic measures to revive their pride and renew the struggle he had built so assiduously over the years.

CHAPTER 6

Ambedkar Reflects

Annihilation of untouchability is my birthright.

*

My social philosophy may be said to be enshrined in three words: liberty, equality and fraternity. Let no one however say that I have borrowed my philosophy from the French Revolution. I have not. My philosophy has roots in religion and not in political science. I have derived them from the teachings of my master, the Buddha.

*

They cannot make history who forget history.

*

Character is more important than education. It pains me to see youths growing indifferent to religion. Religion is not an opium as it is hell by some. I want religion but I do not want hypocrisy in the name of religion.

Freedom and Beyond Manusmriti

THE TRANSFER OF POWER AND PARTITION

The process of the transfer of power began in August 1946, when Nehru was invited to form the Interim Government. The Muslim League refused to cooperate and went on a violent protest, demanding 'Dinia', their sacred land, their Pakistan for Muslims. There were large-scale riots in Calcutta, where the provincial government was headed by the Muslim League. The killings spread to Noakhali which was only a prelude to the partition riots, the most terrible and heinous riots in the history of the subcontinent. In his book, *Thoughts on Pakistan*, Ambedkar had proposed partition and a peaceful transfer of the Muslims and Hindus from their respective regions, in order to avert a civil war. India was now in the midst of a civil war. While the Muslim League pushed for the partition, Ambedkar desperately tried to ensure the interests of the scheduled castes in the future Constitution of India.

AMBEDKAR'S EDUCATIONAL AND LITERARY ENDEAVOURS

Meanwhile, in June 1946, he had founded The People's Education Society, and started Siddhartha College in Bombay, to specifically cater to the education of the scheduled castes. Also, by then, he had published yet another book, namely, *Who Were the Shudras?* In the book, he rejected the idea of racial origin to the development of the caste system, and held the ideology of the Brahmins or Brahminism as being responsible for it. His thesis was that Shudras were originally Kshatriyas and belonged to the Solar Race. After a prolonged conflict between the Brahmins and the Kshatriyas, sometimes also called Dasas or Dasyus, the Kshatriyas were degraded and pushed to the fourth varna which previously did not exist. He also proposed the idea that the untouchables were Nagas, the original Buddhists, who were later degraded by Brahminism which was anti-Buddhist.

The nightmare of partition

The long-awaited Freedom soon turned into a nightmare. The Partition caused unimaginable misery and death leaving behind a trail of blood and bitter memories that continues to haunt India even today.

About ten million people crossed over from Punjab and Bengal; thousands of families were separated, children orphaned, women kidnapped and raped, whole trainloads of dead bodies were exchanged. By the time this terrible exodus finally came to an end, about one million people had perished. Gandhiji, who had declared that the vivisection of the country could be done only over his dead body, became a back number and a horrified spectator of the communal holocaust. When Jawaharlal Nehru unfurled the tricolour national flag, and then later, delivered his now famous 'Tryst With Destiny' speech at the stroke of twelve on the night of 14 August 1947, a dejected Gandhi had gone to sleep early in a remote village. He was to later start on an epic fast unto death to stop the madness and infuse some sanity in the minds of the people.

Ambedkar's warning to Dalits

Ambedkar, worried about the fate of the Dalits, warned, 'I would like to tell the scheduled castes who happen today to be impounded inside Pakistan, to come over to India by such means as may be available to them. The second thing I want to say is that it would be fatal for the scheduled castes, whether in Pakistan or in Hyderabad, to put their faith in Muslims or the Muslim League. It has become a habit with the scheduled castes to look upon the Muslims as their friends, simply because they dislike the Hindus. This is a mistaken view.' And, as an advocate of a strong Central Government, he advised the States of Travancore and Hyderabad, to merge their sovereignty in the Indian Unions, and warned them that to be independent and hope to get recognition and support from outside was to live in a fool's paradise.

MINISTER OF LAW IN INDEPENDENT INDIA

As the head of the new Government of Independent India, Nehru invited Ambedkar to join the new cabinet of Free India as Minister of Law. It came as a great surprise; however, Ambedkar accepted the offer and became the first untouchable Hindu Minister in the Central Cabinet of India. Nehru's offer to Ambedkar says a great deal about not only his political shrewdness, but also his sagacity and objectivity in recognising Ambedkar's worth and his expertise in constitutional matters; just as Ambedkar's acceptance reveals his political pragmatism. However, it should not be forgotten here that Gandhiji stressed the point that the work must be carried on, and the deep-seated animosity has to be transcended.

THE GANDHI-AMBEDKARITE RELATIONSHIP: A DILEMMA

The angry reaction by certain Dalit groups against Attenborough's 'Gandhi' in the 1980s must reflect the dilemma, and the uneasy yet ambiguous relationship between Gandhi and Ambedkarites. The issue could be tellingly illustrated by recapitulating Devanoor Mahadeva's responses and interventions in the matter. Mahadeva is a writer of extraordinary imagination and depth and a leader of great repute in Karnataka. He is one of the founder members of the Dalit Sangarsh Samiti (DSS). In 1982, when the film 'Gandhi' was released in Bangalore, the DSS had protested against its screening, on the ground that it was an insult to Dalits because Ambedkar had been deliberately left out in the story. The absence of Ambedkar in the story was seen as a conspiracy to undermine Ambedkar's personality.

Later, when the film was released in Mysore, the DSS once again planned to boycott the film. Mahadeva was not in favour of the boycott. He was against violence and was worried that the theatre, where the film was to be screened, might be damaged. Some members of the DSS were firmly in favour of the boycott. It was enough, Mahadeva argued, to go on a protest, saying, 'Gandhi without Ambedkar is incomplete'. Later, Mahadeva, much to the ire of his colleagues, went and saw the film.

Reflecting on the film, Mahadeva wrote to the effect that the film portrayed Nehru, Patel and Jinnah as power-hungry characters, and therefore, in a way it was good that Ambedkar had been left out; otherwise he would have been most probably portrayed like another Jinnah. Further, it seemed to him that the script which did not include Vinoba, Lohia, Subhas Chandra Bose and Jayaprakash Narayan could not be construed as an act of conspiracy to harm Ambedkar's image as a Dalit leader. Mahadeva believes that the spirit behind Gandhi's emphasis on

Harijan work was Ambedkar. If he had lived during their period, Mahadeva wonders, who would he have supported? Troubled by this thought, Mahadeva thinks that probably he would have been with Gandhi, but he surely would have argued with Gandhi in favour of Ambedkar. In many ways, this significant revelation by Mahadeva quite vividly captures the Dalit dilemma, and more than hints at the much-needed dialogue between Gandhians and Ambedkarites.

Gandhi was made in South Africa. He was 'made' when he was thrown out of the First Class train compartment, when he was kicked by the White police, when he was treated like a 'coolie'. And through patience, suffering and determination he discovered the weapon of Satyagraha with which he struggled to transform 'the enemy' into a sensitive human being. Ambedkar too believed in non-violence, that is the reason why he ultimately embraced Buddhism, reasons Mahadeva. Non-violence cannot be a mere tactic for Dalit activists because they are in a minority, and they cannot fight against the formidable force of the police and the military. After seeing the Chauri-Chaura incident in the film, in which satyagrahis kill policemen and burn down the police station, when Gandhi withdraws the Non-Cooperation Movement and goes on fast despite opposition from Nehru, Patel and Jinnah, Mahadeva confesses that it changed his opinion about the significance of satyagraha. 'Non-violence cannot be a tactic,' he says with conviction, 'but a way of life.'

The Dalit Movement is at crossroads today. Aggressive forms of protests and violent acts will do more harm than good to the cause of the Dalits. 'Because,' Mahadeva writes, 'Independence has still not come to us. In a way Gandhi's victory over the British was quite easy. In his fight against the enemy who was an outsider, the people of the country were with him. But today we have to win over the intolerant caste Hindus, as we move towards our liberation. Only a handful of caste Hindus might join us in such a struggle. This struggle for freedom, therefore, will be a greater one than the battle fought for political freedom from the British. There are many ways to liberation, and we have to explore them. In this context, Gandhi too might show us a way.'

Quoted from: Yara Japthigoo Barada Navillugalu – A collection of articles about Devanoor Mahadeva's Literature. Edited by P. Chandrika, published by Abhinava, Bangalore, 1999.

ARCHITECT OF THE CONSTITUTION AND 'MODERN MANU'

Now getting back to the main narrative, Ambedkar took up as a challenge the role thrust upon him, the role that would earn him the title of 'modern Manu', who would abolish untouchability and lay the foundation of modern India on the principles of Liberty, Equality and Fraternity, and on Secularism. So now, he plunged back into his work on the Constitution, and in February 1948, completed the draft Constitution and submitted it to the President of the Constituent Assembly.

The Constitution incorporated some of the best and latest features of the major Constitutions in the world. It aimed at the development of a robust nationalism, centralisation, a strong executive, secularism and a welfare State. The executive authority was required to be co-extensive with legislative authority. It stood for federalism, but with a strong Central Government. The equality of opportunity for all citizens was seen as the most important right. The Directive Principles were meant to ensure social and economic democracy, in addition to political democracy. Although Ambedkar had viewed villages as dens of superstitions and caste tyranny, he had offered provision for village Panchayats to enable villages work as local units of democracy. Lastly, the Constitution was modelled more after the

Cabinet System of Government as prevailing in England, than the Presidential form of Government as it existed in America.

HEALTH CHALLENGES AND SECOND MARRIAGE

The long hours of work that stretched into weeks and months for almost two years, ultimately told on his health. He had already been suffering with diabetes. The nights became a nightmare, as pain in his legs increased and left him exhausted by the morning. He took insulin and tried Homeopathy, but found no relief. He was 56 years old now, physically exhausted and had probably begun to feel lonely. He needed a companion and a medical practitioner who would take care of him. He decided to marry Dr Sharda Kabir who had been his personal doctor for some time now. She was a Saraswath Brahmin. There was some opposition from his son and a few other friends. Ambedkar had to settle some financial matters with his son, before he got married to the doctor in Delhi under the Civil Marriages Act on 15 August 1948.

THE CONSTITUTION'S ADOPTION AND ARTICLE 11

After placing the Draft Constitution before the Public for six months, it was introduced in the Parliament by Ambedkar on 4 November 1948. It was a formidable document, biggest compared to constitutions adopted by different countries. It contained 395 articles and 8 Schedules. Each article was taken up, debated over and then adopted. With absolute consensus, Article 11 was adopted, declaring the abolition of Untouchability. When the Anti-Untouchability Act was passed to loud cheering from the benches in the Assembly, it must be noted here, there were also spirited shouts of Mahatma Gandhiji ki jai, Victory to Mahatma Gandhiji. This might sound not merely ironical but like a galling cruel joke today, when we know how hard Ambedkar had worked to draft the Constitution. Gandhiji, we know, was not an advocate of legal measures against untouchability as much as he was for self-purification, for cleansing of the stain of untouchability from the hearts and minds of the caste Hindus, as compared to Ambedkar who had always been for legal abolition of untouchability and had relentlessly worked towards it. Gandhiji's contribution cannot be underestimated here, but the failure to recognise Ambedkar's contribution in the Assembly was more than uncharitable. The recognition did come later, however, and it came without reservation from all quarters. By January 1950, after every article had been discussed and passed, Ambedkar was praised unreservedly from every quarter, both inside and outside the Parliament House.

It was a moment of great historical significance. Here was a man born into a poor Mahar untouchable family, harassed and humiliated by Caste Hindus, who had risen to become a great political leader and a scholar extraordinary, who had fought, struggled and struck back, not with vengeance but with sensitivity and concern, to become the chief architect of the Constitution that would inaugurate a new era in the history of this ancient land. On the final day he rose to a loud cheering and spoke for nearly 40 minutes, in his lucid yet eloquent style, and ended his long speech with a profound warning:

'We are going to enter into a life of contradictions. In politics we will have equality and in social and economic life, we will have inequality ... We must remove this contradiction at the earliest moment, or else those who suffer from inequality will blow up the structure of political democracy which this assembly has so laboriously built up.'

THE HINDU CODE BILL AND RESIGNATION

For about ten years, the Hindu Code Bill had been much discussed and debated over, both inside and outside the government. Ambedkar had revised and submitted it to the Constituent Assembly. It had been his great desire to introduce the Bill. Even Nehru was very keen on it and he had even threatened to resign if the Hindu Code Bill was not passed. The bill relating to the joint family and property rights for women touched a raw nerve. Controversies developed and there were questions regarding the authority of the Assembly which was not an elected body by the people, to pass the bill and impose it on the people. After much quarrel and debate, a truncated Bill was passed which Ambedkar took it as a personal failure and resigned from the Cabinet.

POLITICAL CHALLENGES AND THE REPUBLICAN PARTY OF INDIA

The General Elections was announced in 1952. Many leaders, even from the non-Dalit communities had unreservedly showered praises on Ambedkar as a great constitutional authority, as a scholar with great insight and depth, as not only a champion of the downtrodden, but a great patriot of scintillating character. There had been hints that a time would come when he would be at the helm of the Nation as its Prime Minister. It would have been a crowning glory to his long career and struggle in politics. There is reason to believe that Ambedkar cherished the great desire. But, his Scheduled Castes Federation (SCF) was too small a party. It was weak and lacked strength and discipline compared to other parties, let alone the Congress which he loathed to join. Electoral alliances were tried out with different parties. Ambedkar had discussions with Jayaprakash Narayan and Ashok Mehta. The Peasants and Workers Party (P & WP) including the Hindu

Mahasabha and Janasangh were found to be communal, while the Communists were anti-religious. So the SCF joined hands with the Praja Socialist Party.

The alliance did not work and the SCF had to face ignominious defeat. Ambedkar too was defeated in the Loksabha elections (January 1952). The SCF failure was attributed to its advocacy of the partition of Kashmir, and support to the Bombay Muslims on the issue of separate electorates. Ambedkar, in his campaigns, had laid more stress on the defects of the Congress Governments, rather than proposing effective alternative programmes. He was to face yet another defeat in the 1954 by-election. Although he was a man of remarkable character, intelligence and knowledge, he seemed a poor party leader. It appears that he lacked the ability to make negotiations and build alliances with groups and parties which were not ideologically very different from him. Either he lacked the skill or could not devote enough time to build the party on a solid base, and to groom the second line of leadership from among his co-workers. It was the end of his political career.

It was a great loss to Indian politics, for, given his experience and knowledge he would have been most useful in the Parliament and contributed immensely in the department of Planning or Finance or Commerce and Industry. He could have easily clinched the post of a Cabinet Minister if not become the Prime Minister, if only he had made himself acceptable into the folds of the Congress Party. That was not to be, and refusing to give up, he went on to form a new political party under the banner: Republican Party of India. The name Scheduled Castes Federation (SCF) was changed to Republican Party Of India (RPI) to give it a national look, to widen the scope and character of the party in order to represent the cause of the oppressed and the exploited including the workers, peasants, Dalits and rural poor. The party initially devoted much attention on the problems of the landless labourers, among whom untouchables constituted a major portion. Despite the unexpected death of Ambedkar in 1956, which left the party rudderless for some years, what is noteworthy here is that up to 1964, RPI waged several battles in favour of the landless labourers, and pressed the demand for the distribution of fallow land and wasteland among the landless peasants.

EMBRACING BUDDHISM: A CROWNING GLORY

However, the crowning glory or the great culmination to Baba Saheb's remarkable life would come not in the political arena, but in the religious realm; when finally in 1956 he would embrace Buddhism; when in years to come, in not only Neo-Buddhists conventions, but also in almost all Dalit meetings and conferences, his photograph in Western suit (symbolising modernity) would be placed alongside the picture of Buddha in padmasana, immersed in deep meditation on the sorrow or dukkha of the world, or delivering his discourse on the eight-fold path to good life and liberation.

CHAPTER 7

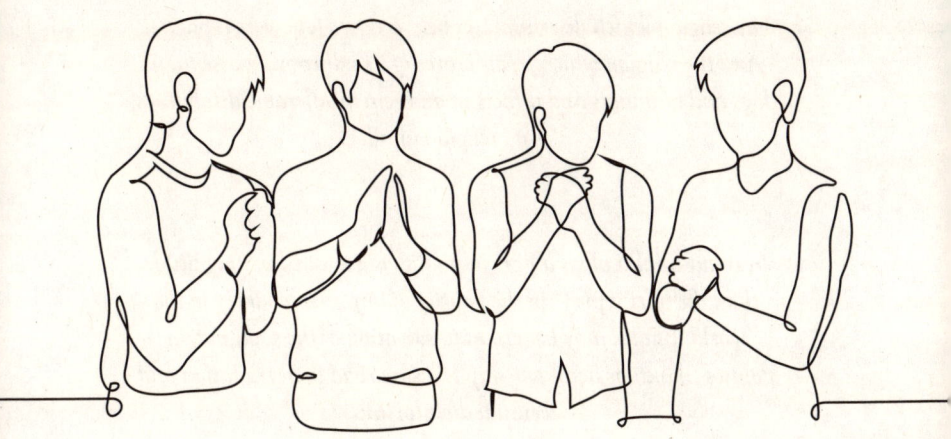

Ambedkar Reflects

A Great Man must be motivated by the dynamics of a social purpose and must act as the scourge and the scavenger of Society.

Carlyle used a happy phrase when he described the Great Men of history as so many Bank Notes. Like Bank Notes they represent gold. What we have to see is that they are not forged notes. I admit that we have to be more cautious in our worship of Great Men. For in this country, we have perhaps arrived at such a stage when alongside the notice board saying "Beware of Pickpockets", we need to have notice boards saying "Beware of Great Men".

*

The religion which discriminates between two followers is partial. And the religion which treats crores of its adherents worse than dogs and criminals and inflicts upon them insufferable disabilities is no religion at all.

In India Bhakti plays a part in politics unequalled in magnitude than the part it plays in the politics of any other country in the world. Bhakti may be a road to salvation of the soul; but, in politics Bhakti or hero- worship is a sure road to degradation and eventual dictatorship.

Refuge in Buddhism and Mahaparinirvana

WHY HINDUISM WAS REJECTED

Time and again, Ambedkar had warned that a religion which discriminated between two followers, which treated crores of its adherents worse than dogs and criminals and inflicted upon them insufferable disabilities, was no religion at all. Mystics and saints had sung songs and propounded doctrines of equality before God, but in actuality all this had not led to any change in the power structure of Hindu Society. Unlike Gandhi, he believed Hinduism could not exist without its chaturvarna, its rigid endogamous caste system. And the destruction of the caste system would be the death of Hinduism, which, now he dismissed as 'a mass of sacrificial, societal, political and sanitary rules and regulations; all mixed up'.

THE APPEAL OF BUDDHISM

Ambedkar was now more than certain that his future lay in the company of Buddha, his refuge in Buddhism. The atheistic tradition, or no-god position of Buddhism appealed to him. There was no authoritarian God, no Big Brother or Almighty Father here looking over the shoulders of his creatures. Buddhism was based on compassion just as it was rooted in egalitarian principles. It taught Prajna (understanding), Karuna (compassion or love towards all creatures), and Samatha (equality between all jivas). No other religion, he reasoned, could be more emancipatory than Buddhism. Moreover it was rooted in Indian soil, and Buddha was looked upon as one of the avatars by millions of Hindus. The conversion in no way would harm the tradition and culture of this ancient land. Further, Buddhism would conscientise the Dalits, lift them out of their marginal existence and place them at the centre of Indian life, giving them a unique historical vocation.

THE HISTORIC CONVERSION CEREMONY

Ambedkar chose Nagpur for the conversion ceremony, where, Nagarjuna, the mystic-scholar of Buddhism, had once lived. An expansive open ground of 14 acres was prepared to hold the historic ceremony. Thousands of Dalits, mostly Mahars, trekked hundreds of miles, singing and shouting slogans: 'Bhagawan Buddha ke jai', 'Baba Saheb ke jai', and reached Nagpur in advance. A huge dais lined with white cloth was installed and Buddhist flags of blue, red and green stripes fluttered everywhere. Streets approaching the holy site were decorated with colour buntings.

On the morning of 14 October 1956, dressed in white silk dhoti and white coat, Ambedkar arrived to loud cheering and chanting, accompanied by his wife in a white sari. To the press reporters he said that once he had told Mahatma Gandhi, that though he differed radically from him on the issue of untouchability and chaturvarna, when the time came for him to renounce Hinduism, he would 'choose only the least harmful way for the country and that is the greatest benefit I am conferring on the country by embracing Buddhism; for Buddhism is a part and parcel of Bharathiya culture. I have taken care that my conversion will not harm the tradition of the culture and history of this land'. When the final moment came, with half a million people watching him with undivided attention, standing beneath a huge replica of the great Stupa at Sanchi, Baba Saheb Dr Ambedkar, in a voice choked with emotions, declared, 'I renounce Hinduism', and embraced Buddhism by way of a simple ritual administered by the 83 year old Mahasthaveer Chandramani of Kushinara and his four saffron-clad Bhikkhus, chanting Buddham Saranam Gacchami; Dhammam Saranam Gacchami; Sangham Saranam Gacchami. Later, as most of the three lakh Mahars stood up, Ambedkar himself administered the three refuges: Buddha, Dhamma and Sangha, the five Precepts and different Pledges.

Fulfilled vows: social reform and new identity

Not long ago, Ambedkar had said, 'if I fail to do away with the abominable thraldom and inhuman injustice under which the class, into which I was born, has been groaning, I will put an end to my life with a bullet'. He fulfilled his vow in two ways:

One, by critiquing and challenging the caste system and Hinduism, he had awakened the conscience of the caste Hindus, and conscientised the Dalits and propelled them into political action, into emancipatory politics by way of self-help, self-knowledge, self-elevation and self-respect. And as the chief architect of the Indian Constitution, he had set in motion democratic forces to transform the caste-ridden, patriarchal Hindu society on the principles of liberty, equality and fraternity.

Two, by embracing Buddhism, he had reconnected the Dalits to one of the most spiritual yet egalitarian traditions of India and given the Dalits a new, energising identity, a new historical vocation.

DETERIORATING HEALTH AND PERSONAL STRUGGLES

Ambedkar was sixty-four years old now. The relentless political activity over three decades had left him exhausted. His failure in the general elections added to his already deteriorating health. He did not smoke nor consume liquor, but his weak constitution was giving away. There were many more milestones to be reached, many more desires to be fulfilled and goals to be achieved; the mind was still active and brilliant as ever, but the body had started sinking. He could not move around without the support of his walking sticks or some person's help. He tried many systems of medicines and healing, overdosed his body with drugs that only led to further breakdown of body resistance. His one-time sharp and penetrating eyes began to fail, and one day, overcome with grief and fear at the prospect of losing his eyesight and not being able to read and write his books, he burst into tears.

AMBEDKAR'S COMPLEX PERSONALITY

Ambedkar was a man given to extreme tempers at times. Humility was not one of his conspicuous merits. He was a proud man, and his sense of pride came from hard toil, his voracious reading and knowledge, his rage against injustices, his tremendous self-confidence to say and do whatever he wished. He was not a very sociable creature if not a thorough introvert, but he could slip into endless, spontaneous conversation with friends, cut hard, crude, country jokes, and laugh loudest of them all. He could be sharp, intense, snappy, biting and vitriolic with words, sometimes with deadly effect, which made some to call him a 'British Bull Dog', and by Sarojini Naidu as 'Mussolini'. But he was a force to be reckoned with, and his words barbed or profound were not to be forgotten easily. Just as he had a passion for books and was a great bibliophile, he had fascination for rich clothes, fine shoes and sandals, grand cars, and even small fine objects such as fountain pens.

REVIVING BUDDHISM AND UNFINISHED WORKS

Now a Buddhist, rather a 'neo-Buddhist' as his followers would be called in future, Ambedkar addressed himself to the task of reviving Buddhism in India. By then he had started working on his magnum opus *The Buddha and His Dhamma*. Also simultaneously he had begun to work on his other unfinished works, such as, *Revolution and Counter Revolution*, and *Buddha and Karl Marx*. There was yet another book, namely, *The Riddle of Hinduism*, which remained unpublished for a long time, and finally when it was published, the book was to become his most controversial work.

BUDDHA AND KARL MARX: A COMPARISON

Although in poor health, Ambedkar attended the World Buddhist Conference at Katmandu in Nepal. Interestingly, during the conference, he was asked to speak on Buddha and Karl Marx. By comparing and contrasting Buddha with Marx, he went on to say that both had the same goal so far as both worked towards the removal of Dukkha or sorrow from life, but they differed radically with regard to the means adopted to achieve the goal. Marxism was based on force, on using violent methods to abolish private property, to usher in equality and social justice, to establish proletarian dictatorship which ultimately made mockery of democracy. Whereas Buddhism, given its philosophy of Impermanence and Dukkha and Nirvana, it was against aggrandisement, against private property as a source of sorrow; and more importantly, the Buddhist path to self-transformation and the transformation of society was based on non-violence, on compassion, which, Ambedkar asserted, was the safest and soundest and yet a revolutionary approach.

Ambedkar saw himself as the Sankaracharya of Buddhism, engaged in the stupendous work for the revival and regeneration of Buddhism. He not only spoke and wrote about the teachings and philosophy of Buddhism, he also simultaneously engaged himself in analysing and laying bare certain schools of thought in Hinduism, how willy-nilly they upheld caste hierarchy and prejudice, and patriarchal values that led to the subjugation of women.

MAHAPARINIRVANA

The book of his life had now reached its last chapter. On 2 December, he attended the celebration of the 2500th Buddha Mahaparinirvana at Bodh Gaya, and met the Dalai Lama. Returning to his residence in Delhi two days later, he worked for long hours and completed the book, *The Buddha and Karl Marx*, and gave it to Rattu for typing. He dictated a few letters to friends and some leaders regarding the steps to be taken to build The Republican Party. The next day, a group of Jain leaders met him at his residence. For some time he discussed certain aspects of Buddhism and Jainism with them. Once they left after inviting him to one of their functions, Rattu began to massage his legs. Rattu not only typed Ambedkar's manuscripts, but served him as his private secretary and attendant. As Rattu pressed his legs, Ambedkar, eyes shut, chanted, 'Buddham Saranam Gachhami'. Then he asked Rattu to play the song on the radiogram. Night had fallen and it was time for supper. He ate a little rice and nothing else. Then supporting himself with his staff, he slowly limped towards his bedroom, humming, 'Chal Kabir tera bhav sagar dera ...' Without bothering to go home, from the previous night, Rattu had stayed by his master's side, attending to his needs. Now lying in his bed, Ambedkar asked Rattu to get him the typescripts of the Preface and Introduction to *The Buddha and His Dhamma*. When Rattu left for his house, it was close to midnight; a light still burned, and close to Ambedkar's cot, stood a thermos containing coffee and a dish of sweets.

On the morning of 6 December 1956, when Ms Savitha Ambedkar came in as usual to wake him up, she found him gone still and cold. His heart, which had grown increasingly weak and feeble over the last two years, had stopped beating.

A NATION MOURNS

Condolence messages poured in from all the prominent leaders. Nehru, the new Prime Minister, sent a wreath through a special messenger. Thousands of people thronged the Alipore Road, and the body was taken on a procession to the airport and airlifted and brought to Santa Cruz, Bombay, at 3 a.m. Thousands of Ambedkar's followers, who had waited through the night, now carried the body in a silent procession to his old residence, Rajagriha, at Dadar. There, several lakhs of untouchables had a last glimpse of their saviour, and thousands, cutting across class and caste, came to pay their last respects to one in whom now they recognised a truly a great man. Schools, Colleges and Cinema halls were closed. Ahmedabad Textile Mills declared a holiday. At noon, the body was placed on a truck decked with flowers and wreaths. Near the head of the body stood a statuette of Lord Buddha. The traffic in the surrounding areas came to a standstill as the procession started with cries of 'Baba Saheb Amar Rahe', 'Dr Ambedkar Amar Rahe'. The nearly two-mile-long procession took about four hours to reach the Dadar Hindu Crematorium. Dusk had fallen and the stars had emerged in the night sky. After the last rites were performed by Buddhist priests, after nearly one lakh people from the Mahar community, from which Ambedkar himself had sprung, embraced Buddhism as a mark of respect to their master and in order to fulfill his last wish, when Yashwantrao lit the pyre, hundreds of miles away at Sanchi, the celebration of the 2500th Buddha Jayanti came to an end.

Ambedkar Reflects

Tell my people, whatever I have done, I have been able to do after passing through crushing miseries and endless trouble all my life and fighting with my opponents. With great difficulty I have brought this caravan where it is seen today. Let the caravan march on despite the hurdles that may come on its way. If my lieutenants are not able to take the caravan ahead they should leave it there, but in no circumstances should they allow the caravan to go back. This is the message to my people.

Epilogue

AMBEDKAR'S LASTING LEGACY

Today, Dr Ambedkar is, quite understandably, seen by millions as one who revived Buddhism in India, as one who set in motion a new socio-cultural revolution. Before he embraced Buddhism, there were about 50,000 Buddhists in the whole of India. Now there are about six million Buddhists and it is a growing community. Ambedkar knew that this society of neo-Buddhists would manage without him, take care of themselves, take care of both their material and spiritual growth in the light of the Dhamma. The Wheel of Dhamma would move again with a new vibrancy, and its followers would throw up alternative, non-violent ways of progress on the social, economic and political fronts, of reconstructing society based on egalitarian principles.

Perhaps he also knew that even after his death, he would continue to be a leader, a living tradition, inspirer of political battles for social justice for the millions of non-Buddhist Dalits in the country. As a matter of fact, the Dalit Movement continues to draw inspiration, strategies and ideas from Ambedkar's life and work for their political struggles, in their efforts to expose caste prejudices, expose collusion of the Law, Police, Bureaucracy, of the landlords and upper castes in the oppression and exploitation of the Dalits, and in their struggles to get land for the landless.

A WARNING AGAINST HERO-WORSHIP

Perhaps Ambedkar also suspected that one day he would be deified and a blind worship of him would set in. Ambedkar hated hero-worship, and was quite critical of the blind adoration of Gandhiji by not only the Congress members. He resented and felt extremely uneasy when his people fussed over him, when he was praised too highly, when he was compelled to preside over programmes, rallies, processions which were organised to felicitate him. In 1932, reflecting on the tumultuous send-off he was given while boarding the ship to London, he wrote that he felt quite restless at such functions, that his frame of mind was more suited to democracy and that he felt quite smothered by such undemocratic displays which smacked of hero-worship.

In November 1948, after every article of the Constitution was discussed and passed, Ambedkar spoke most eloquently about the strengths of the Constitution and the ways of good democracy. At one point, quite significantly, he also spoke about the dangers of hero-worship. Striking a note of warning against uncritical veneration of personalities, he said, 'There is nothing wrong in being grateful to great men who have rendered life-long service to the country; but there are limits to gratefulness. As has been well said by the Irish patriot Daniel O' Connell, 'No man can be grateful at the cost of his honour; no woman can be grateful at the cost of her chastity; and no nation can be grateful at the cost of its liberty.' This caution is far more necessary in the case of India than in the case of any other country. For, Bhakti plays a part in politics unequalled in magnitude than the part in politics of any other country in the world. Bhakti may be a road to the salvation of the soul; but, in politics Bhakti or hero-worship is a sure road to degradation and eventual dictatorship.'

This note of warning needs to be considered not only by the followers of Gandhiji, but also by the followers of Ambedkar in the Dalit Movement. Uncritical acceptance of ideas and hero-worship would only make us intellectually weak, and injure or even defeat our cause. What is of great concern here is a certain lack of creative understanding and appreciation of the anxieties, conflicts and contradictions Ambedkar had to bear while he struggled through four decades, to develop his emancipatory politics in the thick of the struggles against British imperialism, and of rising communal politics of his time. What is of greater concern is the uncritical acceptance of modernity and the sad and counterproductive but questionable and avoidable divide between Gandhiji and Ambedkar.

THE CONVERGENCE OF GANDHI AND AMBEDKAR

Though it may sound like 'irony of ironies', as late D.R. Nagaraj would argue, 'To understand the nature of Babasaheb's political career one has to place it along with Gandhiji's, for the apparent divergence between the two will highlight the unique problems of the former.' According to him, both, Ambedkar and Gandhiji, affected each other deeply and cured each other of their excesses. While the question of untouchability was a civil rights issue and required legal measures against it, to Gandhi untouchability was a problem of the Hindu self, and it needed to be cleansed and transformed inwardly and totally. Although the Self-Purification approach and Self-Respect movement may look to diverge, they do merge at a deeper level and strengthen each other. The exegetical and political, or the political and spiritual, and the moral and legal are not necessarily exclusive and cancel each other, rather they profoundly complement each other.

The intense debate and confrontations between Gandhiji and Ambedkar that spread over more than a decade, changed each other radically. As a result of this, in the words of Nagaraj, 'Gandhiji took over economics from Babasaheb, and Ambedkar internalised the importance of religion.' Gandhiji's Khadi programme, his idea of village swaraj or village reconstruction was geared towards the welfare of village as a whole, but they were intimately related to the problems of the Harijans as well. Eventually, Gandhiji shed much of his ambiguity regarding caste as he realised that 'the evil' was far greater than he had thought it to be, and he unreservedly supported and argued in favour of inter-dining and inter-caste marriage.

Again in the words of Nagaraj, words that come from his deep reflection on and involvement in the Dalit movement of Karnataka over two decades, 'Today there is a compelling necessity to achieve a synthesis of the two (Ambedkar and Gandhi). They clash, quite bitterly at that, at the level of major details, but are complementary at a fundamental level. It is not an easy task to iron out the difference between the two masters, but the necessities of the present are forcing us to see their inner commonality ... In fact, at the level of deeper historical truth the conflicting fact disappears to reveal the underlying truth.'

Mahatma Gandhi's experiments and Babasaheb Ambedkar's trials with truth are far from over. The underlying unity of purpose between the two and the historical necessity of the present should make us realise the need to creatively combine the two approaches, and bring the two masters together as co-workers in the search for an alternative cultural politics in the cause of the marginalised, Dalits, women and rural poor.

Books by Ambedkar

The Untouchables, Who are They? And Why They became Untouchables? Amrit Book Co., Delhi, 1948.

Who were the Shudras? How They came to be the Fourth Varna in the Indo-Aryan Society? Thacker and Co. Ltd., Bombay, 1946.

Buddha and His Dhamma. People's Education Society, D.N. Road, Bombay, 1957.

Annihilation of Caste. Thacker and Co. Ltd., Bombay, 1946.

What Congress and Gandhi have done to the Untouchables? Thacker and Co. Ltd., Bombay, 1945.

Pakistan or Partition of India. Thacker and Co. Ltd., Bombay, 1946.

States and Minorities. Thacker and Co. Ltd., Bombay, 1947. Thoughts on Linguistic States. B. R. Ambedkar, Blind Mahavidyalaya, Aurangabad, 1955.

The Problem of the Rupee: its Origin and its Solution. P. S. King and Sons, Ltd., London, 1923.

The Evolution of Provincial Finance in British India. P.S. King and Sons, Ltd., London, 1925.

The rise and fall of the Hindu women. Dr Ambedkar Publications Society, Hyderabad, 1965.

Emancipation of the Untouchables. Thacker and Co. Ltd., Bombay, 1943.

Maharashtra as a Linguistic Province. Thacker and Co. Ltd., Bombay, 1948.

Dr Babasaheb Ambedkar: Writings and Speeches. Volumes I — XII. Education Department, Government of Maharashtra, Bombay 400032.

BOOKS ON AMBEDKAR

Ambedkar: Life and Mission, by Dhananjay Keer, Popular Prakashan, Bombay, 1961.

Dr Ambedkar and His Movement, by Robbin Jeanette, Dr Ambedkar Publications Society, Hyderabad, 1964.

Thus Spoke Ambedkar, Four volumes, edited by Bhagwan Das, published by Ambedkar Sahitya Prakashana, Ambedkar Memorial Society, Bangalore, 1980.

The Politics of Emancipation, by Dr A. M. Rajashekariah, Sindhu Publications, Bombay.

The Political Philosophy of B. R. Ambedkar, by Dr D. R. Jatava. The Social Philosophy of B. R. Ambedkar, by Dr D. R. Jatava, 1965.

Dr Ambedkar - A Critical Study, by Dr W. N. Kuber, People's Publishing House, New Delhi, 1973.

The Untouchables in Contemporary India, edited by J. Michael Mahar, Rawat Publications, 1998.

Gandhi and Ambedkar-A study in leadership, by Eleanor Zelliot, Tuscon, The University of Arizona Press, 1972.

Buddhist Revival in India – Aspects of the Sociology of Buddhism, by Trevor Ling, 1980. The Macmillan Press, Ltd., HongKong.

Dalit Visions, by Gail Omvedt – Orient Longman Ltd., 1995 New Delhi.

Jai Bhim! – Dispatches from a Peaceful Revolution – by Terry Pilchick, 1988. Windhorse Publications in association with Parallax Press, Glasgow, California.

The Flaming Feet – A Study of the Dalit Movement in India. By D.R. Nagaraj, 1993. South Forum Press in association with Institution for Cultural Research and Action (ICRA) Bangalore.